[redacted]

WILLOWOOD

Also by Cecilia Galante

HERSHEY HERSELF
THE SUMMER OF MAY

WILLOWOOD

By Cecilia Galante

Aladdin

New York London Toronto Sydney

ALADDIN
An imprint of Simon & Schuster Children's Publishing Division
1230 Avenue of the Americas, New York, NY 10020
First Aladdin paperback edition March 2011

Designed by Jessica Handelman
The text of this book was set in Fairfield Light.
Manufactured in the United States of America 0413 OFF
2 4 6 8 10 9 7 5 3
The Library of Congress has classified the hardcover edition as follows:
Galante, Cecilia
Willowood/by Cecilia Galante—1st Aladdin hardcover edition
p.cm.
Summary: Eleven-year-old Lily has trouble leaving her best friend behind and moving to the city when her mother changes jobs, but she makes some very unlikely friends that soon become like family members
ISBN 978-1-4169-8022-3 (hc)
[1. Moving, Household—Fiction. 2. Friendship—Fiction. 3. Schools—Fiction. 4. Pet shops—Fiction. 5. City and town life—Fiction. Down syndrome—Fiction.]
PZ7.G12965 Wil 2010
[Fic] 22
2009018789
ISBN 978-1-4169-8303-3 (pbk)
ISBN 978-1-4169-8591-4 (eBook)

To my brother Herb, who read the very
first—and very bad—rough draft of this book,
and told me that he wanted to read more.
I love you.

Acknowledgments

Although this is the third book of mine to be published, it is the very first one that I wrote. This is the one that stayed in the bottom of my desk drawer for years until, at the suggestion of my agent, the wise and overly capable Jessica Regel, I dusted it off, reworked it, and put it back into her hands. For this, as well as her constant encouragement and never-ending support of all my work, my first thanks go to her.

I would also like to thank everyone at Simon & Schuster for all the effort they put into creating the whole package and making the book look so beautiful. I know there are a lot of you, and I appreciate each and every one. Warmest thanks to my wonderful—and patient!—editor, Ellen Krieger, whose astute suggestions and careful reading made this book what it is today. I couldn't have done it without you.

I have had wonderful readers along the way, without whom I would have been floundering many times over. All my love and appreciation go out to: my mother, Terry Plummer (who also sat in a hot car with me one day while I told her the entire story!); my father, Joseph Plummer;

Donna and Lou Rader; Herbert Plummer; Sarah Galante; Rachel VanBlankenship; Gina Marsicano; Don McMillan; and Rebecca Brown. Very special thanks to Jennifer Weltz, who underwent a mad lightning-brainstorming session with me one afternoon until we came up with the perfect title for this book. You're the best foreign-rights agent any girl could have!

This book was a different book when I first started sending it out in search of a home. It received numerous rejections, all of which hurt. My husband, Paul, was the one who pushed me to continue, who went out in the middle of the night to buy me Chunky Monkey ice cream when the despair reached mountain-peak proportions, and who has, since the day we got married, no matter what kind of day he's having, told me that he loves me.

Without you, baby, none of this would be possible. Thank you from the bottom of my heart.

1

LILY LAY BACK AGAINST HER PILLOW AND listened as her mother spoke into the phone. The pounding downstairs was getting louder. "Yes, of course I've asked them to be quiet!" her mother said. "Several times! And every night there's another problem. . . ."

Lily closed her eyes. How could Mom have thought that moving to the city would be a good thing? Their lives had been so perfect back home in Glenview, where everything was quiet and green. At night Mom would open the windows so the breeze could drift in, and Lily would fall asleep to the sound of crickets chirping. Here in the city, she was surrounded by steel and sirens and car horns. Mom had opened the window a little bit their first night, since it was so warm, but it had been too loud to sleep.

"Don't worry," she'd said, sliding it shut again. "We'll get used to it." Lily had rolled over and squeezed her eyes shut. She knew it wasn't Mom's fault that she had been let go from her job. And she was pretty sure that her mother realized by now how upset she was about having to leave her best friend, Bailey. But she wasn't about to pretend everything was going to be okay, like Mom was constantly doing. It wasn't okay. And she didn't know if it ever would be again.

She tried not to cry as she thought about Bailey for the umpteenth time. Bailey had been her best friend since the first day of kindergarten, when they'd discovered they were wearing the exact same shoes. Lily smiled as she remembered the expression on Bailey's face when she looked down and saw that Lily had on identical pink and white princess sneakers with Velcro straps. They had worn them all year, even when the heel of Bailey's had gotten ripped and the Velcro strap on Lily's left shoe had stopped working.

She and Bailey looked alike too. Once a girl at the mall had asked if they were twins. They had looked at each other, giggled, and then said yes. Other than the fact that Bailey was at least four inches taller than Lily, they really could pass for twins. Or at least sisters. Their light brown hair was cut just below their ears, and they both had wide blue eyes and small noses. They even had the same ears, tiny and shaped like pink question marks. The best thing about Bailey, though, was that she wasn't boring. In fact, Lily never knew what was going to happen when they spent time together. Bailey, it seemed, had a way of turning perfectly ordinary days into something magical. Take their tree, for instance. To Lily it had been just another willow tree next to the empty tennis courts in the park. It had a brown trunk and branches with leaves. Big deal. But one afternoon, as Lily and Bailey cut through the park on their way home from school, Bailey stopped in front of it.

"What's the matter?" Lily asked.

Bailey cocked her head and then bent over, as if looking at the tree upside down. "What are you doing?" Lily asked. It was getting close to six. Mom had dinner on the table every night at six fifteen sharp. Lily was not allowed to be late. "Come on, I have to go."

Instead of answering, Bailey walked straight toward the tree. "Bailey!" Lily called. "I'm gonna be late!" She watched her friend disappear through the leafy curtain of low-hanging branches.

"Get in here!" Bailey's voice drifted out from inside the tree. "You won't believe this!"

Lily walked toward the tree and yanked aside the branches. *"What?"*

"All the way," Bailey said, beckoning with her fingers. Her voice was soft. "You gotta come in all the way." Lily sighed and stepped through the opening. It wasn't a very large space, especially since most of it was taken up by the trunk. But as the branches slid back into place, she became aware suddenly of standing in a pool of golden light. All around them, like an enormous umbrella, the flat yellow leaves formed a perfect wall, shutting out the rest of the world. It was so quiet that Lily could hear Bailey breathing in and out next to her.

"Whoa," she said.

"Look up," Bailey whispered. Lily tilted her head back. Through the tangle of limbs and branches, little patches of pale blue sky peeked through. But otherwise, Lily thought, it was like being inside an upside down jar of honey. "It's like a whole other world inside here, isn't it?" Bailey said.

"Uh-huh," Lily answered.

They named it Willowood and met there every day after school, unless the weather was bad. Bailey found a rusty beach chair in her basement that her mom said she could have. The spring was broken in the back, but if they leaned it against the trunk, it worked just fine. When Lily's Aunt Wava, who lived in New York City, sent her a postcard of the *Alice in Wonderland* statue in Central Park, Lily poked a hole through the top of it and threaded it through one of the tendril-like branches. Those were her favorite times with Bailey, when they would lie listlessly on the beach chair, staring up at the postcard, which swayed like a forgotten photograph among the leaves.

A few months later, Mom came home with the news that she had gotten a new job. Lily was excited to see Mom so happy; it had never been a secret that Mom hated her job waitressing, and now she said she was going to make a lot more money. But then she let it drop that the job wasn't in Glenview. It was four hours away in a city called Riverside Heights. Lily had heard of Riverside Heights once on the news. Someone had been killed there. The body had been found the next morning by a man who was fishing. Of course Mom didn't seem to take this bit of information very seriously when Lily reminded her of it.

"I know it's a big change, honey," was all she said. "But it'll be okay. I really think you're going to like it."

Knock, knock, knock!

Now, Lily pulled the covers up to her chin as Mom rushed to the front door. Outside her window, flashes of blue and red blinked through the blackness.

"You Mrs. Sinclair?" a deep voice asked.

"*Miss* Sinclair," Mom said. "Yes."

Lily rolled her eyes. Mom always corrected people when they assumed she was married.

"Did you make the complaint?" the voice asked.

"Yes, I did," Mom said. "Right downstairs . . ."

Thud, thud, thud.

The noise interrupted Mom midsentence.

For a second, Lily wondered if maybe someone else in Riverside Heights was getting murdered. Right beneath them.

"You hear?" her mother said. "Did you hear that? That's been going on all night!" Her voice drifted off as she followed the policeman down the steps. Lily could hear him banging on the door downstairs.

"Open up! Police!"

Lily rolled over.

Of course Mom thought she knew what she was talking about when she told Lily that she was going to love Riverside Heights.

Adults always thought they knew everything.

2

LILY'S NEW SCHOOL WAS CALLED Riverside Heights Elementary. It was so big that when Lily looked down the hallways, she couldn't see the end of them.

Now, Lily sat up straight in her seat as Mrs. Bing swept into the room. Mrs. Bing was her new fifth-grade teacher. She reminded Lily of Olive Oyl: tall and skinny with black hair that she pinned back into a bun. She wore the same flat purple shoes every day, with little white flowers on the sides, and red lipstick that was always, *always* smeared along her front teeth. She also blinked. A lot. Especially if she got mad or worried about something. Then her eyelids would start fluttering up and down like crazy, almost like there was something stuck in there.

"Let's get started on our essay presentations, class," Mrs. Bing said. She spoke in a high-pitched, singsong kind of voice. "I'm very interested to hear what you did over the summer. And of course, how you've expressed yourselves through your writing."

Mrs. Bing seemed to be very hung up on the way her students *expressed* themselves. Especially on paper. She'd even talked about it on the very first day of school, when she told the students they were going to be writing an essay every week. Lily wasn't big on expressing much of anything—especially to people she didn't even know.

"Who would like to go first?" asked Mrs. Bing. A few hands went up in the air, but Amanda Peterson waved hers so hard back and forth that it was impossible not to notice. "Okay, Amanda," Mrs. Bing said. "You may begin."

Amanda tossed her long blond hair over her shoulder and pranced up to the front of the room. Lily sat back glumly. Aside from her annoying voice, which made her sound like she had just inhaled a helium balloon, Amanda Peterson's only conversations throughout the day seemed to revolve around what new expensive thing her parents had just bought her.

"This summer," Amanda said, pausing dramatically to look around the room, "my parents took me to Paris." There were a few stifled gasps from the front of the room, where Amanda's best friends sat, but Lily rolled her eyes. Who cared? She blew a mouthful of air through her lips and started in on her daily shoe check.

Except for heels—which Mom wouldn't let her wear yet—there was rarely a shoe Lily came across that did not catch her attention. Lily had a *thing* for shoes. She thought that shoes, maybe more than anything else, said a lot about people. Like what they wanted to be when they got older. Or if they wanted to try a little bit of everything until they found the perfect fit. Lily had six pairs in her own closet, ranging from pink polka-dotted flats to brown boots with rubber lug soles. She chose specific shoes for specific days, according to how she felt. For the last two weeks, since she had been in Riverside Heights, she had worn nothing but her black sneakers with the electric orange shoelaces. And she had no plans—at least in the immediate future—to change that.

Jonathan Finster and Clive Bergen, who sat in the front of the room and did everything together, including getting into trouble, had on identical red basketball sneakers. Jonathan's laces were untied and hung down loosely on the floor. Clive's laces had been carefully double-knotted and tucked in behind the tongue. Margaret Haggerson, who was already five foot eight and usually wore basketball sneakers, had on a pair of navy blue flats today. They were cute, except for the wide black bow that ran across the front. Lily wasn't big on bows. She counted eight more pairs of sneakers—one with no laces at all—two pairs of dirty flip-flops, and one pair of brown leather loafers.

The loafers, each of which had a shiny copper penny in the top, belonged to Gina Soo, who sat directly in front of Lily. Gina was Mrs. Bing's favorite student. Her long dark hair, pale skin, and small eyes, which were hard to see behind her big brown-framed glasses, made her look like a supernerd. Gina got all A's and had at least forty sharpened pencils lined up inside her desk. Every morning, as Lily came into the room and sat down behind her, Gina said hello. Lily said hello back, but she was only being polite.

Amanda began to talk about some dumb museum called the Loove, going on and on about all the boring paintings and statues she'd seen there. Lily put her head down on the desk. She wondered what Bailey was doing right now. Because it was long distance, Mom allowed her to phone Bailey only on Wednesdays and Saturdays. The last two times Lily had called, Bailey had not been around. Last Wednesday she had been at some girl's house, and on Saturday she had been at her Girl Scouts meeting, which Lily had forgotten about.

"Lily?" She picked her head up when she heard her name being called. Mrs. Bing was blinking like mad. "Are you all right, Lily? You don't feel ill, do you?" Mrs. Bing was constantly asking people if they felt all right, ever since Greg Basham threw up all over his desk on the second day of school. Lily shook her head. Amanda had stopped reading. She looked over at Lily and wrinkled her nose. "Okay, then, sit up straight, please. And pay attention," Mrs. Bing said.

"*Any*way," Amanda said, tossing her head. "I really think everyone should go to Paris at least once in their life. It really is the beautifulest city in the world."

"Sweet!" Clive yelled, clapping loudly. "Go, Paris!" Mrs. Bing raised her eyebrows in Clive's direction and then wrote his name on the board. Mrs. Bing was very strict about people yelling out in class. If a student talked without first raising his hand, she put his name on the board. If it happened again, she put a check after his name and had him stay after school. When a person received three checks, it meant detention and a call home.

"Thank you, Amanda," Mrs. Bing said now. "Your essay was excellent. There was a slight mistake right at the end of your presentation, however."

Amanda blinked. "There was?"

"Can you tell me where you've read the word 'beautifulest' before?" Mrs. Bing asked.

Amanda sniffed. "In the dictionary."

"Really?" Mrs. Bing's eyelids fluttered.

Amanda nodded uncertainly.

"I'm sorry, Amanda, but that word would most definitely not be in the dictionary," Mrs. Bing said. She turned to look at the rest of us. "Can anyone tell me what Amanda should have said instead of 'beautifulest'?"

Gina raised her hand hesitantly.

"Yes, Gina?" Mrs. Bing asked.

"Most beautiful," Gina answered. She kept her eyes on her desk as she spoke.

Amanda threw a hateful look in Gina's direction.

"That's right, Gina," Mrs. Bing said. "Thank you. You may take your seat now, Amanda." Amanda plopped down at her desk, making a big show of crossing her legs to show off her boots. They were very high, almost up to her knees, and had buckles around the ankles. Even from where she sat, Lily could tell the soft leather they were made of was expensive.

"Lily?" Mrs. Bing asked. "I'd like you to go next, please." Lily felt her stomach flip-flop. She swallowed hard, feeling the blood rush up the sides of her face, and walked to the front of the room. Her paper trembled in her hands. "Go ahead," Mrs. Bing encouraged. "We're listening." Lily coughed once and began:

"This summer I moved. My mom got a new job and

we came here in the middle of August. I don't really like it. Our apartment gets really hot and we don't have air-conditioning. I went to the Coal Street pool a few times, which is only a few blocks away from our apartment building, but it's kind of boring. We also have vampire neighbors who stay up all night and make a lot of noise, so it's hard to sleep."

She paused, studying the next line, which read *I miss my best friend, Bailey, more than anything,* and then looked over at Mrs. Bing. "That's it."

Mrs. Bing blinked and blinked. "That's the whole essay?"

Lily stared down at her neon shoelaces. For a split second she thought how cool it would be if all the lights went out and the only thing anyone could see was her shoes.

"Um hmm," she said.

"Well." Mrs. Bing looked thoughtful. "That's a good start, Lily. But it would be a lot better if you put some detail into it." She paused "How about the pool, for example? What did the water feel like?"

"The Coal Street pool is for scums!" Jonathan Finster yelled out. "All the kids pee in it!" The room erupted with laughter.

"Jonathan!" Mrs. Bing said sharply. She glanced at

the board, where his name, along with a check mark, was already written. "That kind of language is forbidden in my classroom. You will stay after school with me this entire week."

Jonathan slumped against his desk. "Well it's *true,*" he muttered.

"Can I sit down now?" Lily pleaded.

Mrs. Bing nodded. "Thank you for reading, Lily. For our next essay, I'd like you to remember what I said about details."

Lily rushed back to her seat. Her ears were so hot, she wondered if they were bright red. Out of the corner of her eye, she saw Jonathan lean over toward Clive. He kept his beady eyes on her as he spoke out of the side of his mouth.

"I thought she smelled kind of funny," he whispered. "Now we know why." Clive laughed and gave him a high five.

Lily stared straight ahead at the back of Gina's head. Her long black hair was twisted into a complicated French braid. It hung down between her shoulders like the rope they had to climb in gym. Lily wondered if Gina braided it herself, or if her mother did it for her. Mom didn't know how to braid.

Neither did Lily.

3

AFTER THE FINAL BELL RANG, LILY GOT on the D-4 bus. It had taken her a few days to get used to the fact that there was more than one bus—and that she had to find it at the end of the day. Back in Glenview there had been only one bus for the whole school. Lily didn't know the bus driver's name on D-4, but she secretly called her the Freakazoid. She was a tall, skinny woman with frizzy black hair. Every day, no matter what, the Freakazoid had a pair of orange earbuds stuck in her ears. The volume was turned up so loud that Lily could hear the clash of screaming music whenever she walked by. Sometimes, as she drove, the Freakazoid pounded the heel of her hand on the steering wheel, jangling a horde of silver bracelets that hung around her wrist.

The bus was full of kids, but Gina, Amanda, and Clive were the only people Lily knew so far. Gina always sat in the very first row, directly behind the steps. Her stop was first, and when the bus screeched to a halt on her corner and the Freakazoid yanked open the doors, Gina made sure she was the first one off. Lily usually found a spot on the left side, toward the back, and scooted up next to the window.

It had begun to rain. Lily pressed her forehead against the glass and stared out at the gray surrounding her. She hadn't minded the rain back in Glenview. It made everything look even greener, and when it was over, a lilac smell filled the air. Here in Riverside Heights, the rain made everything look and smell dirty.

"You think you're so smart, don't you? Correcting me like that in front of everyone?" Amanda's voice was coming from the front of the bus. She had moved from her seat in the back and now was sitting directly behind Gina, jabbing her in the shoulder as she spoke. "Can't you even look at me when I'm talking to you? Huh?" Gina kept her head down. Her long braid disappeared behind her hunched shoulders.

Lily glanced over at the Freakzoid. She was jutting her chin in and out, in and out, to the music blaring in her ear buds. Lily felt queasy as she watched Amanda lean over the seat and whisper something in Gina's ear. She wondered if she should say something. Gina obviously wasn't going to retaliate in any way. But she stayed put. It wasn't like she was Gina's friend. And the last thing she needed right now was some bully like Amanda on her case.

Amanda brought a compact up to her face and stared at herself in the mirror. She licked a finger and then drew it across one of her eyebrows. Lily looked away, trying to ignore the bad taste that had started to climb up the back of her throat.

The bus lurched to a halt. Gina stood up immediately. She clutched a pile of books against her chest with one hand and readjusted her backpack with the other as she waited for the Freakazoid to open the doors. Lily waited a few seconds, staring out the window. Gina always crossed in front of the bus and then came around to the left side of the street where, Lily guessed, she lived nearby. Lily squinted as Gina appeared suddenly, hoping she was just imagining it, but she knew she wasn't. Even behind Gina's glasses, she could see tears sliding down her face.

Lily had to walk half a block to get home, and she made sure to step on every single crack along the way. It was something she and Bailey used to do—just to be different. Today, she pretended that each crack was Amanda's back.

Lily walked up the little walkway in front of their building and opened the heavy wrought-iron door. Two men carrying a couch almost knocked her over.

"Watch it!" one of them yelled. She stepped quickly to the side and started up the steps, turning sideways so she could watch. The men angled the couch out the front door and staggered down the front steps. Lily turned around quickly and pushed her way inside her apartment.

"Lily?" Mrs. Hiller's voice came floating out from the living room. She had the TV on. Dr. Phil was on the screen, talking softly to some lady who was crying her eyes out.

Lily dumped her knapsack on the floor next to the door. "Yeah, it's me." She walked into the living room and sat down on the old green couch. Mrs. Hiller lived across the hall in 2B. She was chubby, in a nice sort of way, and had short white hair. She had come over the very first day, when Mom and Lily were moving in, and brought them a zucchini-carrot cake, covered with cream cheese icing.

Mom had been delighted when, after some small talk, Mrs. Hiller told her she would be happy to watch Lily after school. Mom always said that good babysitters were harder to come by than two-dollar bills. Lily didn't know why Mrs. Hiller automatically qualified as a good babysitter just because she had raised six children of her own and had ten grandchildren. But that seemed to seal the deal for Mom. Now, Mrs. Hiller watched Lily every day after school, until Mom came home from work.

"What's going on with the vampires downstairs?" Lily asked.

Mrs. Hiller adjusted a pile of yarn she was knitting in her lap. "The vampires?" she repeated.

Lily shrugged. "That's what Mom calls them. I guess 'cause they're always up at night."

Mrs. Hiller laughed. "Well, that's as good a name as any for those folks."

She had on her soft blue slippers with the round pom-poms on the front. Lily had never seen her wear anything else.

"Are they moving out?" Lily asked.

"They are indeed," Mrs. Hiller said. "I guess enough people complained about the noise they were making. The landlord was here yesterday, talking to them. He must've told them they had to go." Her silver knitting needles clacked as she moved them back and forth. "*Now,* apparently."

"Well, Mom will be happy." Lily stood up and stretched. She was happy too, but she didn't say that. "I'm gonna go check on Weemis."

"Pick up that knapsack!" Mrs. Hiller called out behind her. Sometimes Lily wondered if Mrs. Hiller had eyes in the back of her head.

Her sneakers made a peeling sound as she walked across the floor and grabbed her knapsack. Mom had gone nuts over the floors when they first looked at the place. She said she had always wanted to live in a place that had hardwood floors. Lily couldn't understand what Mom was so excited about. For one thing, the floors were slippery. When she walked around in her socks, she was always sliding and catching herself on a piece of furniture. And if she had to get up to go to the bathroom in the middle of the night, the floor was so cold underneath her bare feet, she had to tiptoe.

She sat down at the foot of her bed and peeked into the plastic terrarium on her bookshelf. The terrarium had pink gravel on the bottom, a tiny water dish, and a small foam rock in the corner. Weemis, who lived inside the terrarium, was her pet gecko. He was tiny and green and adorable, but that was not the main reason Lily loved him. The main reason Lily loved him was that when she talked to him, she knew Weemis listened. Whenever she came over and sat down in front of his terrarium, he would crawl on top of his foam rock and stare at her. Without Bailey, he was the only one who listened to the stuff she didn't want anyone else to hear.

Today, though, when she peeked inside his terrarium, he was asleep under the foam rock. His tiny tail was curled around his body. Lily sighed. She had wanted to tell him about Amanda. Instead, she made her way into the kitchen.

A blue plate filled with cubed yellow cheese and apple chunks sat in the middle of the kitchen table. Lily pretended she didn't see it.

"What are you looking for?" Mrs. Hiller called out as Lily began opening and closing cupboards. "I've got a nice cheese and fruit platter all set out for you!" Lily grunted and pulled a bag of Doritos out from behind a bag of flour. She couldn't be sure, but she was starting to think that Mrs. Hiller was hiding all her favorite foods.

Mrs. Hiller was not a fan of things like Doritos and Froot Dots. Every day, when Lily got home from school, the same blue plate was set out on the kitchen table. If it was a vegetable day, the blue plate might be filled with celery sticks, carrot coins, cucumber chunks, or red pepper slices. If it was a fruit day, slices of apples, oranges, or pears, or clusters of grapes would be piled on the plate. Last Tuesday, there was a strange little purplish-red fruit that Mrs. Hiller called a pluot. She said it was a combination of a plum and an apricot.

Lily had tried one of the carrot coins once, just to be polite. But it didn't have any *taste*. It was like eating crunchy water. She tried to point out to Mrs. Hiller that her Sooper-Grape Froot Dots were, in fact, made out of fruit. "Look," she said, pointing to the box. "It says right here. 'Made with *real* grapes.'"

Mrs. Hiller smiled. "Oh no, dear. They're not the same thing at all."

Lily couldn't tell what the difference was, but she wasn't about to argue with Mrs. Hiller about it.

Now, spying a jar of peanut butter, she grabbed it. Luckily for her, Mrs. Hiller did not consider peanut butter to be as evil as Doritos or Froot Roll-ups. She did, however, frown when Lily dug it out of the jar with her fingers. To avoid a scene, Lily took a teaspoon from the silverware drawer and scooped out some peanut butter. She sat down at the table and closed her mouth around the spoon. The salty and sweet tastes filled her mouth like glue. Heaven.

"How was school, dear?" Lily's eyes flew back open as Mrs. Hiller sat down across from her. Lily never heard her coming, since her slippers didn't make any noise on the wood floors. Mrs. Hiller reached out and pulled the plate of apple slices closer. She popped a cube of cheese in her mouth.

"Pri-ee goo," Lily answered, trying to pry the peanut butter off the roof of her mouth.

"Didn't you see the beautiful fruit platter I made for you?"

Lily nodded and swallowed her peanut butter.

Mrs. Hiller sighed. "Anything interesting happen in school?"

Lily thought about her essay. She shook her head. "No."

"Your mother called. She has to work late tonight."

"Again?" Lily let her mouth fall open. This was the third time Mom had had to work late. "Man, that sucks."

Mrs. Hiller drew her eyebrows together in a narrow line. "Lily, what did I tell you about using that kind of language?" Her voice was soft but stern.

Lily flushed and nodded. It was pointless to tell Mrs. Hiller that she heard that word at least a hundred times a day at school.

Mrs. Hiller cleared her throat. "Besides, you didn't let me finish. Your mother wants you to call her. She said she has a surprise for you."

4

LILY FELT A PRICKLE OF EXCITEMENT AS she raced to the phone. Maybe Mom had gotten some time off. Maybe they were finally going to go back to Glenview so she could visit Bailey.

"Mom?" she said breathlessly. "What's up? Mrs. Hiller said you had a surprise for me!"

Mom laughed. "Hello to you too, pumpkin. How was your day?"

"Mo-oo-om! What is it? Tell me!"

Her mother laughed again. "Okay, sweetie, relax." She cleared her throat. "You know how long Aunt Wava has been working to try to get an exhibit, right?"

Lily frowned. Aunt Wava? What did Aunt Wava have to do with Bailey?

"Yeah?" she said uncertainly.

"Well, she called me this morning, Lil, and told me that she finally got one! Can you believe it? After all this time! A real art exhibit of her own!"

Lily knew all about exhibits, since that was pretty much all Aunt Wava ever talked about when she came up to visit them. She knew that getting an exhibit to show artwork in a place like New York City was a big deal, since there were about a million other artists there, all trying to do the same thing. But right now, it didn't seem like a very big deal at all.

"Lily?" Mom's voice sounded through the phone. "Are you still there?"

"Yeah."

"Well, why don't you sound more excited, honey? Don't you know how important this is?"

"Yeah, I know."

"Well, I haven't even told you the best part." Lily held her breath. "We're going, Lily! To see the show! New York City, honey. Our first trip. Finally!"

"Oh," Lily said.

"Lily, what is it?" Mom asked. "I thought you'd be jumping around like a monkey."

Lily swallowed a lump in her throat. "I thought you were gonna say I could go see Bailey." She tried to steady her words. They were coming out all wobbly.

"Oh, Lil," Mom said. She sighed deeply. "Honey, we'll go back. I promise. I just have to get enough time under my belt to request some time off."

"Well, how're you gonna get time off for Aunt Wava's show?" Lily challenged.

"That's not for another two months. I'll have the time by then."

"Two months?" Lily repeated. "Why so long?"

"It takes a while to get these things all set up, I guess," said Mom. "Aunt Wava didn't really say."

Lily suddenly thought of a great idea. "Can Bailey come with us?" She didn't give her mother time to answer. "Oh, please, Mom? Pleasepleasepleaseplease?"

Her mother sighed again. "Oh, sweetie, no. Not this time."

"Why? Why not?"

"For one thing, it would take a lot of juggling to get Bailey to our place and then back home again after the trip. Remember, we're four hours from Glenview now. It's not like I can just go pick Bailey up around the corner."

"But . . ." Lily stopped as she heard the click of a lighter and then the tight sound of Mom inhaling. "Are you smoking?"

Her mother exhaled loudly. "No."

"Yes you are. I can hear you."

Mom exhaled again. "No, I'm not." There was a shuffling sound over the phone. "Okay, I was," Mom said. "But I just stubbed it out with my toe. Okay?"

"You always tell *me* not to lie," Lily said.

"I know," Mom answered. "I'm sorry." She paused. "Listen, we're gonna have the greatest time in the world in New York City. I promise, okay? Just you, me, and Aunt Wava. It's gonna be a blast." Lily didn't answer. A siren sounded in the background. Mom sighed. "Honey, I have to go. We'll talk more about this later. Try to cheer up, okay? And make sure you eat everything that Mrs. Hiller makes you for dinner. Oh, and ask her to double-check your homework too, okay? Bye, honey. I love you."

She hung up the phone so fast that Lily didn't get a chance to say the word "but," which was poised on her lips like a tiny pearl. For a moment she just sat there without moving. She wondered if Mom had rushed off the phone so fast so she could go have another cigarette. She had promised Lily over and over again that she was going to quit, but she never did. She didn't smoke in the house anymore, at least, but Lily knew that she probably made up for lost time when they were apart.

She could hear Oprah on TV in the other room, talking about the truth. Lily got up slowly and walked into the kitchen. She wondered if Oprah had ever done a show on parents who didn't tell the truth to their kids.

She plugged the electric teakettle into the wall, got out her favorite mug with the pink gecko on the front, and filled it with two teaspoons of instant decaffeinated coffee. Thankfully, Mom had put her foot down with Mrs. Hiller when it came to Lily drinking coffee. She had two cups every day, no matter what.

Mrs. Hiller walked back in as Lily was stirring in the vanilla-flavored cream.

"Well, what was the surprise?" she asked.

Lily shrugged. "Nothing, really. My aunt got an art exhibit in New York City and we're going to see it."

Mrs. Hiller sat down at the table and crossed her arms. Her brown cardigan sweater was unraveling at the cuffs. "Well, I wouldn't call taking a trip to New York City *nothing*. That's one of the most exciting cities in the world."

Lily didn't answer.

"What kind of art does your aunt do?" Mrs. Hiller asked. She pronounced the word "aunt" like "ont."

Lily stared at her coffee as she stirred it with her spoon. It was turning into a little whirlpool. "I don't know. Trees and stuff. And people's faces."

"Ah, a portrait artist," Mrs. Hiller said, nodding. "How lovely."

"Yeah." Lily picked up her mug and took a sip. Mmmm.

The first sip of coffee was always the best. "I'm gonna go in my room and call Bailey."

Mrs. Hiller cocked her head and narrowed her blue eyes. "Homework done?"

"I'll do it later," Lily said. She walked slowly so that she wouldn't spill the coffee.

"You know your mother's rule," Mrs. Hiller said, clicking her tongue. "No phone calls until you do your homework."

Lily dropped her head back between her shoulder blades. A scream blocked the center of her chest. "Please?" She turned around. "Just this once?" Her eyes were getting wet with frustration.

Mrs. Hiller frowned. "Lily." Her voice was soft. "What is it, dear?"

Lily shook her head. She knew that if she said another word she would start crying and she did not, under any circumstances, want to cry in front of Mrs. Hiller, who would probably launch into some kind of Dr. Phil or Oprah speech. She stared down at her coffee instead. "Okay," Mrs. Hiller said suddenly. "Just this once, dear. But then you must do your homework."

Lily looked up. "Thanks," she whispered.

She dialed Bailey's number, holding her breath as it began to ring. The scream inside her chest had eased a little.

"Hi, Mrs. Sewell," she said as Bailey's mother picked up the phone. "This is Lily. Can I talk to Bailey, please?"

"Hel*lo* Lily!" Mrs. Sewell answered. "How are things going in the city? Do you like it?"

"It's okay," Lily said, hoping she didn't sound impatient. Mrs. Sewell was a very nice woman, but she liked to talk. A *lot*.

"Oh, good! And how about your new school? Do you like it? I'm sure it's a huge adjustment."

"Yeah, it's pretty big."

"About how many kids are in your classroom now?" Mrs. Sewell asked.

Lily rolled her eyes. "I don't know, exactly. Maybe thirty?"

"Really?" Mrs. Sewell made a clucking noise with her tongue. "My, that must take some getting used to. You know, Shirley Carverton just moved, and so Bailey only has eleven kids in her class now."

"Is Bailey there?" Lily asked. She was starting to feel a little desperate.

Mrs. Sewell sighed. "Actually, no, honey. She's still at soccer practice."

"Soccer?" Lily repeated. She'd never even heard Bailey mention soccer in the past. When had that started?

"Yes," Mrs. Sewell answered. "I was a little surprised

myself, Lily, when she told me. But it seems as though a few girls have convinced her that she's goalie material."

Lily didn't know what to say.

"Would you like me to have her call you back?" Mrs. Sewell had asked this question both times before when Lily called and Lily had said yes. But Bailey hadn't called her back.

"Um, no, that's okay," she said now. "Just tell her I'll try again on Saturday."

She hung up the phone and put her head down on the bed.

There was a knock on the door.

"All finished?" Mrs. Hiller asked.

"Mpf," Lily answered against the bedspread.

"Dinner will be ready in an hour," said Mrs. Hiller. She paused. "Time for homework now, Lily."

"What're you making for dinner?" Lily asked.

"Chicken stew," Mrs. Hiller answered. Lily wrinkled her nose. "And homemade biscuits with butter," Mrs. Hiller added.

Biscuits she could do. Especially with butter. Stew anything sounded pretty iffy. Lily rolled over and grabbed a notebook out of her knapsack. For their essay this week, Mrs. Bing had told them to write about their favorite subject in school. Lily stared at the ceiling for almost twenty minutes, chewing on the eraser at the end of her pencil, before she thought of anything to say.

I don't have a favorite subject in school, she wrote finally. *Maybe if there was a class about shoes, I would, but since there isn't, I don't.* She stuffed the paper into her English folder. She knew it wasn't even half of what Mrs. Bing expected, especially when it came to details, but she didn't care.

She had bigger things to worry about.

Like whether her best friend in the world cared if she was alive or dead anymore.

5

BAILEY WAS AT A SLEEPOVER ON SATURDAY.

The rest of the week didn't go very well, either.

On Monday, as Gina made her way over to her desk, Amanda stuck out her foot and tripped her. Mrs. Bing was still in the hallway, talking to another teacher. Gina's books, which she had been holding tight to her chest, flew across the room like a stack of cards. Gina followed, hurtling face first into a desk. Her glasses scuttled across the floor. Kids screamed with laughter. Jonathan and Clive pointed at Gina and high-fived each other. Lily, who was drawing a picture of wedge shoes with satin crisscross straps in her notebook, kept her head down and pretended not to notice.

For snack after school, Mrs. Hiller tried to get Lily to

eat half a grapefruit. She had sliced it down the middle, loosened the segments, and even sprinkled a little bit of sugar on top. But Lily shook her head. She wasn't even that hungry. She had two cups of coffee instead.

On Tuesday, Mrs. Bing handed back everyone's essay. Lily received a D. Underneath the grade, in neat red letters, Mrs. Bing had written: *Shoes are not a school subject. Next time, please answer the prompt.* Lily caught a glimpse of Gina's essay over her shoulder. The bright red A stood out like a stop sign.

Snack was celery sticks filled with peanut butter. Mrs. Hiller was trying to get creative, Lily thought as she licked out the peanut butter and left the empty celery sticks on the blue plate.

On Wednesday, they had gym. Mr. Finkelsteiner, the gym teacher, wore shorts that were too tight, white tube socks that came up to his calves, and green basketball sneakers. He blew his whistle a lot and scratched his arms. He was also very competitive, turning everything the students did into some kind of contest. The dodgeball tournament they started today, for example, was going to be whittled down to two final players, who would then have a face off against the rest of the class. There could be only one winner in the championship game, Mr. Finkelsteiner said, and he wanted every student to try his or her hardest to be that person.

Lily had never admitted this—not even to Bailey—but dodgeball terrified her. Having to maneuver her way in the middle of a circle, while trying to avoid a ball being thrown at her like a cannon, made her sick to her stomach. She and Bailey had always managed to convince their gym teacher at Glenview to let them sit out on the benches whenever they played dodgeball. But that was not a possibility with Mr. Finkelsteiner.

Lily stood in the middle of the circle, her shoulders hunched around her ears, trying to make herself invisible as the players on the outside began to fire the ball. She was clocked almost immediately by Owen Tougher, who seemed to sense her fear. She took her spot on the outside of the circle, relieved to be out, rubbing the spot on her leg where Owen had zinged her with the ball. Gina, however, was a totally different story. Lily watched openmouthed as Gina zigzagged around and behind and through everyone like a water bug skating across a lake. The rules required that the ball not be thrown any higher than knee level, and Gina's feet moved like quicksilver, leaping over the ball and scissoring wide when it veered in her direction, threatening to knock her off balance.

Suddenly Clive, who had already gotten nailed by

someone, fired the ball directly at Gina. It was much too high. She leaned back, but underestimated the ball's height. It slammed against her ear. Gina dropped like a rock. Her glasses went flying, spinning along the slick gym floor like a windup toy.

Mr. Finkelsteiner blew his whistle and waved his hands. "Time out!" he screamed. Gina sat up slowly, looking dazed. Blood trickled from her lower lip. Behind her, Clive gave Amanda a thumbs-up. She winked at him.

"You!" Lily looked up as Mr. Finkelsteiner pointed at her. "Yeah, you!" he barked. "Go with Gina to the nurse."

"Bye, baby!" Clive yelled, cupping his hands around his mouth. "Make sure you get a Band-Aid for your boo-boo!"

"Quiet!" Mr. Finkelsteiner shouted. "That was an illegal play, Bergen! Take a seat!" He blew his whistle as Clive sulked across the floor toward the bleachers. "Let's go! Back to the game!"

Lily walked silently beside Gina as they made their way down the hall. She'd never been in the hallway when it was empty. The blue linoleum floor was so dirty that their sneakers left footprints. She hoped Gina knew where she was going, because she had no idea where the nurse actually was. She glanced sideways at Gina, who was holding her hand against her mouth.

"You okay?" she asked softly.

"No," Gina snapped. "I'm not okay. I'm *bleeding*."

Lily stared straight ahead. The blue lockers looked like soldiers standing in line on either side of them. She guessed Gina was mad at her, although she didn't have a reason to be, since Lily hadn't done anything wrong. "Do you know where you're going?"

"Yes," Gina answered. She pointed to a red door across the hall that read NURSE on the front. "And you don't have to come with me, you know. I'm perfectly capable of doing this on my own."

"Well, Mr. Finkelsteiner—"

"My glasses!" Gina interjected. She clutched at her face. "My glasses! I left them in the gym!" She turned around. "I have to go back. Amanda'll do something to them if I don't . . ."

Lily grabbed her arm. "I'll go get them," she said. "Come on, you gotta let the nurse look at your lip. I'll go get your glasses."

Gina's shoulders sagged a little.

Lily squeezed her arm. "I'll be right back, okay?"

The glasses were in Mr. Finkelsteiner's shorts pocket. He must have been expecting Lily to come back for them, because he held them out to her without a word as she approached. "Gina okay?" he asked.

"Yeah," Lily answered. "She's all right."

That night, Lily tried to call Bailey three times. The line was busy.

On Thursday, Gina kept her eyes on the floor as she walked into the classroom. She stepped carefully around Amanda's white patent leather flats and took her seat. There was a thick piece of masking tape around the middle part of her glasses. They sat unevenly on her face, like a lopsided rectangle. Her lower lip was swollen with a tiny split down the middle. She didn't look at Lily, but Lily glanced over as Gina opened her desk. Next to the row of perfectly sharpened pencils were ten pink rubber erasers, a neat stack of small notebooks, and another pile of larger notebooks. Gina pulled out one of her small notebooks with the words DAILY LOG on the front cover. Encircling it with her arm, she put her head down and began to write. A little while later, during social studies, Gina yawned and lifted her arms. A folded-up piece of paper dropped out of her hands onto Lily's desk.

Lily unwrapped it carefully, keeping her eyes on Mrs. Bing. Writing notes meant an automatic check after your name on the board.

Thanks for yesterday, the note said. *I really appreciate it.*

Mom had to work late again on Friday, but she gave Lily permission to call Bailey so she wouldn't have to wait another whole day. Lily dialed the phone, trying to pretend that she didn't care whether or not Bailey was home. But when Bailey picked up the phone this time, Lily's heart almost leaped out of her chest.

"Bailey! It's me! Where've you been? How come you haven't called me? It's been, like, forever!"

"Yeah." Bailey's voice was flat. "I know."

Lily frowned. "So what's up? How are you? How's school? Do you like it? Is it hard?"

"Geez, Lily, slow down." Bailey sounded annoyed.

"Well, tell me, Bay! Tell me!"

Bailey took a deep breath. "Well, my mom told you I joined soccer, didn't she?"

"Yeah, she did." Lily refrained from saying anything critical. She wasn't sure why Bailey was acting so strange, but she didn't want to do or say anything to make it stranger.

"It's really awesome. I love it. Coach Benning says I'm really fast."

"That's great," Lily said.

"And I joined cheerleading too."

"Cheerleading?" Now Lily really was puzzled. Hadn't Bailey just told her last year that she would be a cheerleader when it snowed pink snowflakes? "Why?"

"What do you mean, why?" Bailey sounded indignant. "Because it's fun, that's why. You should try it."

"I don't know," Lily said. "But I know I won't try out for cheerleading until it snows pink snowflakes." She held her breath, waiting for Bailey to recognize the remark.

"Yeah," Bailey answered instead. "Well, you never know if you like something until you try it."

There was a brief, awkward pause.

"So," Bailey said at last. "When are you coming back for a visit?"

Lily smiled and breathed a sigh of relief. She knew the old Bailey would come to the surface eventually. "Prob'ly really soon. My mom has to work double shifts for a while, because she's new, but she said we could come to see you in a few weeks." Lily stepped hard on her toe. She knew she shouldn't lie.

"Oh," Bailey said. "Well, let me know when you know for sure, okay? Trisha Wheatley invited me to her parents' cabin at the lake next—"

"Trisha *Wheatley*?" Lily repeated, horrified. Trisha Wheatley was at least six inches taller than any other student at Glenview Elementary and she had buck teeth that stuck out of her mouth like a jack-o'-lantern's. As far as Lily could tell, Trisha was bored, because there was no reason whatsoever for the mean things she did to everyone, including Lily and Bailey. One time, she shoved Bailey into a locker. Another time, she "accidentally" bumped Lily in the lunch line, scattering her French fries all over the floor. Bailey had told Lily to ignore her, and that she would stop eventually. But she hadn't. On Lily's last day at Glenview, Trisha Wheatley had thrown a Tootsie Roll at her as she was getting off the bus. It had hit Lily in the cheek and, because of the force of Trisha's throw, had left a mark.

"Yeah, Trish Wheatley," Bailey repeated. "What's wrong with that?"

"W-w-we can't stand Trisha Wheatley!" Lily stammered.

"*We,*" Bailey said slowly, "are not a 'we' anymore, Lily, in case you didn't notice. And *I* happen to like Trisha Wheatley. She's the one who told me to try out for soccer. She's nothing like she used to be. People can change, you know."

"Tell me about it," Lily said.

"What's that supposed to mean?" Bailey snapped.

"Since when did you start liking soccer and cheerleading and Trisha Wheatley?" Lily demanded.

"Since you left," Bailey retorted. "Since I had to find other friends and other things to do."

Lily felt her heart sink. "Just because I'm not there doesn't mean we can't be friends, Bailey. You're my best friend." She paused. "In the whole world."

"Yeah." Bailey's voice was softer. Lily could hear her cracking her knuckles over the phone, which was something Bailey always did when she was nervous. "It's just that things are so different now." She sounded sad too.

"Bailey?"

"Yeah?"

"How's Willowood?"

There was no answer.

"Bailey?"

"Yeah. I heard you." Bailey inhaled deeply. "They cut it down, Lily." A ringing started in Lily's ears. She opened her mouth, but the only thing that came out was a squeak. She thought she heard Bailey say something about the Glenview park people having to make room for more tennis courts, but she couldn't be sure.

"So it's gone, then?" Lily's voice sounded hollow.

"Yeah," Bailey said. "I'm sorry. I know how much it meant to you."

To us, Lily thought furiously. *It meant a lot to us.*

"I have to go," Bailey said. "My mom is calling me downstairs. I'm sorry."

Lily swallowed hard. For some reason, it felt as if this was going to be the last time she ever talked to Bailey.

"Okay," she said. "Bye, Bailey."

6

LILY SHUT THE DOOR TO HER ROOM and lay down on top of her purple comforter. She placed her coffee mug on top of her shirt, where it made a little circle of warmth against her belly, and stared up at the ceiling. Between the white paint and the sun coming through her window, she could barely make out her plastic glow-in-the-dark stars. At night, though, when Mom turned out all the lights, the stars glowed above her like a miniature sky.

Once, when she had spent the night over at Bailey's, they had stayed outside until it was so dark they could barely see each other. It was a warm summer evening. The air smelled like charcoal grills and fresh-cut grass. She and Bailey had lain down in Bailey's front yard and stared up at the heavens. She remembered feeling very, very small underneath all those stars, and for a moment, it frightened her. Then, without a word, Bailey had reached out and taken her hand. It was one of Lily's favorite memories.

She doubted if Bailey remembered it. Now that Bailey was hanging around Trisha Wheatley all the time, there was no way she'd remember anything about their friendship at all. How did things like that happen, she wondered. How, after six years together, could she have been so easily replaced?

She sat up and put her mug on the bookshelf next to Weemis, who was still sleeping. Reaching inside her pillowcase, she felt around until her fingers came in contact with the picture.

It was of her father. He was sitting on a swing, his hands gripping both sides of the chain-link handles, blue sneakers high up in the air. His mouth, which showed a chipped front tooth, was open wide in an enormous grin. Lily brought the picture closer to her face and studied it. Her eyes roved over every detail, including part of a tattoo that peeked out from underneath the sleeve of his T-shirt, and the way his sideburns came down past his ears. Even the tree in the background, which was green and full of leaves, was a clue. It must have been a summer day, she thought.

She wondered who had taken the picture. It must have

been Mom. How else would it have ended up in the bottom of Mom's jewelry box? That was where Lily had found it three years ago—completely by accident. She had been looking for a pair of clip-on earrings to wear to school, since Bailey was wearing hers, and had seen the corner of the picture sticking out from beneath the blue velvet. She hadn't needed to ask Mom who it was; something about his smile told her right away it was her father. Two seconds later, she had the picture hidden inside her pillowcase, where it had been ever since.

Now she rolled over so she was lying on her stomach. She thought back to the day in first grade when her teacher, Miss Snow, had asked all of her students to draw pictures of their families. Lily had been so excited. She loved to draw. She drew herself first, wearing a purple dress and shiny green shoes. Next came Mom, whose hair was still long back then. Lily put a bow on top of Mom's head and gave her a pink dress and heels. She hadn't gotten Weemis yet, so he wasn't in it, but she drew an enormous rainbow over the whole thing and colored it in. She wrote the words *My Family* on top of the picture and gave it to Miss Snow.

After lunch, all the students gathered around the Art Wall to study their finished projects. Lily was admiring hers when Stanley Winterbottom suddenly yelled out, "Hey Lily, how come you didn't draw your dad?" Lily frowned and began to look at the other pictures more carefully.

Stanley Winterbottom was right. Hers was the only picture without a dad in it. Even Nancy Klinefelter, whose parents were getting divorced, had drawn her father—even if he was way over on the other side of the paper.

That night at dinner she had asked Mom about it. They were in their old apartment, eating Lily's favorite meal—fish sticks dipped in mayonnaise, mashed potatoes with yellow gravy, and canned corn.

"Mom?"

"Hmmm?"

"Why don't I have a dad?"

Mom stopped chewing, although a muscle in her left cheek moved. "You do have a dad," she said. "I've told you this before, Lily. He just doesn't live with us."

Lily knew very well that she and her mother had had this discussion. But now she wanted some more answers. "Why not?"

Mom rolled a few pieces of corn around on her plate. "He just . . . doesn't." She took a deep breath. "He left right after you were born."

"Why?"

"I'm not really sure why."

"Where is he now?"

Mom shook her head. "I don't know."

"Why not?"

Mom gave Lily a sideways look. She did that a lot when Lily asked too many why's. "Because he didn't tell me."

So far, none of Mom's answers were any different from those in the previous conversations they'd had about this situation. Lily decided to try a different tactic. "Do you remember what he looked like?"

Mom looked out the window at the big apple tree in their backyard. It was full of soft pink blossoms. "He was tall," she said finally. "Much taller than me. Black hair. Brown eyes."

"Was he handsome?"

Mom grinned. "What do you know about handsome?"

"Was he?"

"Yes. He was."

"Where'd you meet him?"

"At Ruby's." Ruby's was the place where Mom waitressed.

"Did he work there too?"

"No, he was just a customer. A regular for a while."

"What did he order?"

"To eat?"

"Yeah."

"I don't remember what he ordered, honey. It was kind of a long time ago."

"But you said he was a regular."

"Ummm . . ." Mom leaned her head back against her chair. "Let's see. He liked vanilla milkshakes. Meatloaf. French fries."

Lily wrinkled her nose. "I like chocolate milkshakes."

"I know you do," Mom said.

Lily didn't say anything for a few minutes. She was trying to get a picture in her head of what her father looked like sitting in one of the red booths at Ruby's, drinking a vanilla shake. It wasn't as easy as she had hoped.

"Mom?" she asked again.

"Hmmm?"

"What's my dad's name?"

"Reginald, honey. Reginald Worthington."

Lily's last name was Sinclair.

She frowned. "Well, why'd he leave?" she asked again. "Why didn't he—"

"I don't *know* why," Mom cut her off gently. She shook her head and then wiped her mouth with her thumb and index finger. "I already told you, honey, he just did. Sometimes people don't give you reasons." She stood up. "Listen, honey, do you want some more fish sticks? There's plenty here." She scooped a few more onto Lily's plate without waiting for her to answer, and then opened the kitchen door.

"*Mom . . .*"

The door led outside to a tiny back porch. Mom reached into her back pocket and pulled out a package of cigarettes. "I know, I know," she said, closing the door a little. "I'm gonna quit. I promise."

When she was in third grade, during one of Aunt Wava's visits, Lily decided to ask her about her father. They were at Itgen's, the little ice cream shop on the corner, sharing a peanut butter sundae. Mom was still at Ruby's, finishing up her shift.

"Did you know my dad, Aunt Wava?"

"Your dad?" Aunt Wava repeated, as if she hadn't quite heard correctly.

"Yeah," Lily answered. She dug her spoon down deep into the sundae glass, where the peanut butter sauce was still hot. "Did you ever meet him?"

"Uh, a few times," Aunt Wava answered. "Not enough to really know him, though." She put her spoon down and ran her hands over her head. Aunt Wava had wide, massively curly hair, almost like a clown's. When she was little, everyone in her family called her Wavy Wava. She cut her hair all the time, but it grew back like a weed, hanging in tangles and coils around her pretty face. Mom said that Aunt Wava's hair looked like a rat's nest.

"I want to know things about him," Lily said.

"Have you asked your mom?" Aunt Wava asked.

"Yeah. A few times when I was in first grade."

"And what did she say?"

"She said he was handsome and that they met at Ruby's." Lily put a teaspoon of whipped cream into her mouth. It felt like a tiny pillow against her tongue. "I haven't asked her since then, though. She got upset, I think. She went out to smoke afterward."

Aunt Wava held up the maraschino cherry. "You gonna eat this?"

"Nope," Lily answered.

Aunt Wava popped the cherry into her mouth and chewed. "Well, I only met him once or twice," she said. "I remember he told me to call him Reggie. He was tall . . ." She held up her hand as if to touch the ceiling. "Probably over six feet."

"Wow," Lily said. "That is tall."

"And he had nice hair," Aunt Wava continued. "You know, black with a sort of salt-and-pepper look to it."

"Salt and pepper?"

"That's what they call it when someone has little bits of gray in their hair."

"Ewww!" Lily said. "Was he old?"

Aunt Wava laughed. Her teeth were stained pink from the maraschino cherry. "No, goofball. Some people just get gray in their hair when they're young." She paused and put one finger against the side of her nose. "I remember he had a very distinctive-looking nose. There was a big bump in the middle of it. I think he may have broken it at one point and never got it fixed."

Lily put a spoonful of vanilla ice cream inside her mouth and let it melt along her teeth. It was easy to get a picture inside her head listening to the way Aunt Wava described him. She didn't want her to stop. "What else?" she asked.

"Hmmm. I think he had a tattoo on his arm."

"Like yours?" Aunt Wava had a tattoo of a Siamese cat on her left shoulder. She had gotten it after her cat, Salvador Dalí, died of leukemia. She also had a tattoo of a rose on her leg, and a crescent moon on her stomach.

"I don't remember seeing it up close," Aunt Wava said. "But I don't think it was a cat."

"Why didn't he stay with us?" Lily asked.

Aunt Wava stared at Lily for a few seconds. Her eyelids were coated with pale purple glitter. They sparkled in the light. "That's something you need to ask your mother, sweetheart."

"I already did." Lily stared down at the table. "She said she didn't know."

"Well, if she doesn't know, then I'm sure no one else

does." Lily looked up as Aunt Wava made a weird noise. Her tongue was stuck all the way out of her mouth.

There, in the middle of it, was the stem from the maraschino cherry, tied into a perfect knot.

It had been almost four years since Lily had talked to Mom about it; two since she had talked to Aunt Wava. And now, all this time later, Lily thought, she still wasn't any closer to finding out the real answer as to why her father didn't want anything to do with her.

She didn't realize she was crying until she heard Mrs. Hiller's voice outside her door. "Lily, dear?" A soft tap sounded. "Are you all right?"

She shoved the picture under her pillow and wiped her face with the heels of her hands. "Yeah, I'm fine."

The door opened a crack. "Can I come in?" Lily didn't say anything as Mrs. Hiller padded into her room and sat down on the edge of her bed. She rubbed her back. "Why are you crying, dear? What's wrong?"

The questions made Lily cry harder. She buried her face into her pillow and shook her head. "Nothing." There was no way she was going to talk to Mrs. Hiller. She wouldn't understand.

"It certainly doesn't seem like nothing," Mrs. Hiller said. "Sometimes, if you talk about things . . ."

"No," Lily said into the pillow. "I don't want to talk about anything."

Mrs. Hiller was quiet for a few moments, although she did not stop rubbing Lily's back. It felt nice. "I have an idea," she said finally.

Lily sniffed and waited.

Mrs. Hiller tapped her shoulder briskly. "I want you to get up, wash your face, and come with me."

"Where are we going?" Lily asked, raising her face a few inches away from the pillow.

"You'll see." Mrs. Hiller stood up and walked across to the door. "Come along, dear."

7

LILY TRIED TO KEEP PACE WITH MRS. Hiller as they walked down Ivy Street, but it was hard. Mrs. Hiller moved very fast. She had changed out of her blue slippers into a pair of brown shoes with tan laces. They were worn and scuffed at the toes, with thick rubber soles. Definitely old-people shoes.

The September sun hung like a small orange behind one of the tall silver buildings ahead. The downtown area was only three blocks from their apartment. Mom and Lily had been downtown twice since they moved here. It was okay. There were a bunch of department stores, two delis, and a coffee place called Mr. Bean that had a big waterfall in front of it.

"Where are we going?" Lily asked now, hoping Mrs. Hiller would turn around.

"Right this way," Mrs. Hiller replied, pointing ahead with her index finger. "We're almost there." Lily tried to keep up as they passed an enormous department store. The plastic mannequins in the window were wearing winter hats and coats. She could see Mr. Bean over on her right and the waterfall, which for some reason looked smaller today than she remembered.

"Here we are!" Mrs. Hiller said, stopping halfway down the next block. Lily ran to catch up with her. Mrs. Hiller opened a door with the words PET PALACE on the front and walked inside. The scent of wet fur, cat pee, and sawdust filled Lily's nostrils. She stepped around a group of plastic palm trees and stared. Dark green grape-leaf vines were strung so thickly across the ceiling that it was hard to imagine a ceiling existed at all. Birdcages of all different sizes hung down from thick chains. Lily could see bright blue and green wings flapping inside, and dry scaly feet skittering along the wooden perches. The entire right wall was enclosed by a sheet of glass. Behind the glass in various compartments were all sorts of small, furry animals: hamsters, gerbils, white mice, and ferrets. Some were asleep atop mounds of shredded sawdust, others amused themselves inside red plastic wheels.

"This way, dear!" Mrs. Hiller called, striding down an aisle. "I have something special to show you!" Lily followed reluctantly. She wished Mrs. Hiller wasn't always in such a hurry. "Bernard!" Mrs. Hiller called out as they reached a wall of fish tanks.

A large man in front of the fish tanks turned around. "Elaine!" he said, smiling wide. He had a thick black mustache and a belly that protruded so far out in front of him that it looked as if he had swallowed a basketball. A furry little object was perched on his shoulder. Lily blinked and then squinted as the object moved.

It couldn't be.

Was that a *monkey*?

"Where've you been?" the man asked, hanging a small blue net on a metal hook. He put an arm around Mrs. Hiller. "We haven't seen you in a while!" The object on his shoulder stood up on its hind legs suddenly and screeched. Lily took an enormous step back.

Mrs. Hiller laughed. "Hello to you too, Duke!" She reached out and grabbed the monkey's paw. The animal screeched again, a high, screaming sort of sound that made Lily wince. He had big eyes set against a white face with black markings. His long tail, which reached down almost to the man's belt, curved at the end, like a question mark. A tiny blue sweater covered the top half of the monkey's body, and his feet were so small that at first Lily could hardly see them at all.

"I want you to meet a special friend of mine," Mrs. Hiller said, putting her hand on Lily's shoulder. "This is Lily Sinclair. She lives right across the hall from me. Lily, this is Bernard Stump. He owns the store."

"Nice to meetcha, Lily Sinclair," Bernard said. He pumped Lily's hand up and down. Without warning, the monkey on his shoulder stood up again. He cocked his head, looking at Lily with his big eyes. Then he extended his hand, as if to shake. Lily stared, dumbfounded. "Good boy, Duke!" Bernard said. He turned his attention back to Lily, who hadn't moved. "This here's Duke. Don't worry, he's just trying to be polite. He won't bite." Lily took a step forward and extended her first finger. The monkey grabbed it with his tiny paws and yanked it toward his mouth. Lily jerked her hand away and bolted backward, almost knocking Mrs. Hiller over.

Bernard laughed. "He doesn't know what to do exactly, after he takes your hand," he explained. "But he won't bite it. I promise." Lily watched the little animal as he settled back on Bernard's shoulder and glared at her. She wasn't so sure about that.

"Lily's a lizard fan," Mrs. Hiller said.

"Oh yeah?" Bernard asked. "We got a few of those

here." He headed toward the cash register at the front of the store. "Let me take care of this guy and then you can take a peek."

A few minutes later Bernard led them into the Reptile Room. It was off to the side, separated from the center of the store by a small door. Lily stopped in her tracks as she came face-to-face with a glass terrarium at the front of the room. Inside sat two yellow lizards the size of large watermelons. Scaly skin, the color of cold butter, covered their bodies, and when they blinked, their eyelids closed like tiny window shades.

"These here are my iguanas from South America," Bernard said. "This one's Butch." He pointed to the one with triangular spikes running up and down its back. "And this is Beatrice." Lily took a step closer to look at the female. She was smaller than Butch and didn't have any spikes. She was also sleeping. "Beatrice sleeps a lot these days," Bernard said. "She's going to be laying eggs soon. Nate and I have to make her nesting cage pretty soon."

"What's a nesting cage?" Lily asked.

"It'll be her own special place," Bernard answered. "Away from Butch here. Laying eggs is a very stressful thing for an iguana. They need as much space and privacy as we can give them."

"Where is our Nate, by the way?" Mrs. Hiller asked.

Bernard grunted and tipped his head back. "Nate!" he bellowed. "Hey, *Nate*! Get on out here!"

Lily could hardly talk as she let her eyes rove around the rest of the room. The Glenview Pet Corner at the Glenview Mall, where Mom had bought Weemis for her, had been so tiny, she could barely remember it. They'd had geckos, a few mice, and some hamsters. That was all. Bernard's store was like something out of a dream. Everywhere she looked, a different type of lizard looked back: chameleons, anoles, blue-tongued skinks, even a real bearded dragon.

"Hey, Mrs. Hiller!" Lily turned as a strange, hollow-sounding voice rang out behind her. There was a man at the end of the aisle, hugging Mrs. Hiller. Something about him made Lily feel weird inside—although she didn't know why. He was much smaller than Bernard and he seemed unbalanced, almost as if he might tip over as he stood there. His baggy blue jeans, *Superman* T-shirt, and brown sneakers didn't look unusual, but the red winter hat lined with brown fur sure did. The hat had long flaps with silver snaps at the ends that hung down loosely over his ears.

Mrs. Hiller patted the man on the back. "Hello, dear," she said. "My, you look fine." She gestured to Lily with her arm. "Come here, Lily. I want you to meet another good friend of mine."

Up close, Lily could see the man's eyes. They were shaped like almonds and they slanted up. His face was too flat, as if someone had pushed against it—hard. She didn't know what was wrong with him exactly, but she knew what kinds of names people called someone who looked like him. Retard. Idiot. Moron. Her face turned pink thinking of it.

"This is Nate," Mrs. Hiller said. "He's Bernard's son. He works here too. Nate, this is Lily. She lives right across the hall from me."

Nate peered curiously at Lily with his small eyes. "Do you want to buy a cat?" he asked.

Lily shook her head, confused.

Mrs. Hiller laughed. "Nate is in charge of all the cats here," she said. "He's always trying to sell someone a kitty." She squeezed Nate's shoulder. "Aren't you, Nate?"

"Cats are the best," Nate said. His voice was too loud, as if he were speaking to Lily from across the room. "They're *sneaky*." He paused. "I like that."

Lily swallowed. Cats made her nervous *because* they were sneaky. Bailey had one named Minx who used to creep up behind Lily whenever she was over watching television and then pounce on her, as if Lily were a great big mouse. Bailey thought it was funny, but Lily screamed every time.

"Lily's favorite animal is the lizard," Mrs. Hiller continued. "She has a pet gecko at home."

Nate scrunched up his face. "Lizards are boring."

"Well, Lily doesn't think so." Bernard gave Nate a look that said he wasn't pleased with his remark. He flicked his hand toward the door. "Go on, Nate. Get back to work."

Nate scowled and looked sideways at his father. Then he lifted his hand. "Good-bye, Mrs. Hiller." His eyes flitted toward Lily. "Bye."

"Good-bye, dear," Mrs. Hiller said. "I'll see you soon."

"So you wanna hold this bad boy?" Lily stared at Bernard as he unlatched the top of the iguana cage and reached for Butch.

"Hold him?" she repeated. "Seriously?"

Bernard chuckled as he lifted the scaly animal with both arms. " 'Course I'm serious. Butch loves to be held." Lily took a step back as he moved toward her, holding the iguana. It was one thing to hold Weemis, who was the size of a string bean. Butch was about the size of a newborn baby. What if he wiggled? "It's okay," Bernard said encouragingly. "He won't wiggle. He likes it. I promise."

Lily opened her arms as Bernard lay the reptile inside them. His scaly skin felt like sandpaper against her fingers. She stood very still, hardly daring to breathe.

Suddenly, the animal turned its bony head and looked directly at her. He blinked slowly, as if he had all the time in the world.

"You see?" Bernard chuckled. "You're a natural."

"The Lizard Lady," Mrs. Hiller said fondly.

Lily grinned.

8

DO YOU WANT TO SIT WITH ME AT LUNCH *tomorrow?*

It was another note from Gina. Underneath the question Gina had drawn two squares. Next to one was the word *yes.* Next to the other was the word *no.*

Lily thought for a while, nibbling on the end of her eraser. She wondered whether checking *yes* meant that Amanda and Clive and Owen would start giving her a hard time. And she'd not only have to deal with them during lunch but on the bus as well, since the Freakazoid had gotten new headphones that were even louder than the old ones. Then again, the only other person in this school aside from Mrs. Bing who had said more than two words to her was Gina. And she was getting tired of eating lunch all by herself every day.

Quickly, before she changed her mind, she checked the box marked *yes,* and dropped the note back over Gina's shoulder.

Lily didn't know why she was surprised by what was in Gina's lunch box. When she thought about it later, she couldn't imagine Gina eating any other way. But now she stared as Gina unpacked a small plastic container and placed it in front of her. Inside was a mess of what looked like cold spaghetti, green and red pepper strips, shaved carrots, and peanuts. Some sort of brown sauce collected in the corners of the container, like dirty dishwater. Gina twirled a wad of noodles around her fork, dabbed the whole thing into the dishwater sauce, and inserted it into her mouth.

"What *is* that?" Lily asked. They were sitting at the end of a table near the soda machine. Five or six other kids that Lily had never seen before sat on the other side of the table, laughing and eating.

"Pad thai," Gina answered.

"Pad *what*?"

"Pad thai." Gina pronounced the second word "tie." "It's just noodles and vegetables. My mom made it last night." She pushed the container across the table. "Wanna try some?"

Lily leaned back. "Uh, no." She paused. "I don't really eat stuff like that."

Gina took another bite. "Stuff like what?"

"Uh . . . you know. Vegetables and . . . things."

"Your mom doesn't make you eat *any* vegetables?"

"Well, some." Lily took a bite of her peanut butter sandwich. It looked so plain next to Gina's spread. "I mean, we have carrots and peas sometimes." She paused. "And canned corn. That's about it."

Gina shrugged. "I've always eaten stuff like this. I like it. But maybe that's because I don't know any different."

Lily eyed the rest of Gina's lunch box contents. There was a green apple, a bottle of water, and an M&M cookie as large as a tricycle wheel. "Did your mom make that cookie too?" she asked enviously.

Gina shook her head. "Nope. My dad. He's a really good baker. He makes a different kind of cookie every day."

Lily raised her eyebrows. "Your *dad*?"

"Um hmm." Some of the dishwater sauce dripped down Gina's chin. "You can have half of it, if you want. I can never eat the whole thing."

"Oh, okay." Lily tried not to sound excited. "If I'm not too full."

They chewed in silence for a few moments.

"So what'd you get on your favorite subject essay?" Gina asked.

Lily grunted. "Mrs. Bing said I didn't answer the prompt, so she gave me a D."

"Well, maybe she'll let you do it over," Gina said. "Mrs. Bing is pretty fair."

"I don't want to do it over," Lily muttered. "I'm no good at writing." She wondered how long it would take Gina to finish her noodle thingy. That cookie really looked good.

"I love to write," Gina said.

"Not me."

"I could help you." Gina paused, looking at Lily over her glasses. "If you want, I mean."

Lily started to decline, but was stopped by a flying French fry. It hit her squarely in the forehead, leaving a small, oily spot above her eyebrow. Gina gasped. There was a shriek of laughter on the other side of the cafeteria. Lily looked over. Amanda was doubled over, holding her sides, as her group of friends howled along with her.

Lily stood up, although she didn't have the faintest idea what, if anything, she was going to do. All she knew was that after putting up with Trisha Wheatley's nastiness, she wasn't about to spend another year getting bullied.

"Lily." She looked down as Gina grabbed her arm.

"Don't," Gina said. "Please. Just ignore her." Lily felt her fists loosen. Relieved, she sat back down and unclenched her teeth. Her hands were shaking.

Gina was staring at her empty noodle container. Little shreds of carrot littered the bottom. "You don't have to sit with me tomorrow," she whispered finally.

Lily shoved the rest of her sandwich into her paper bag. She slurped the rest of her Hi-C, crushed the box, and put that into the bag too. Then she balled the whole thing up and held it between her hands. "But then I won't get to try your cookie tomorrow," she said. "Different one every day, right?"

Gina raised her eyes.

Lily was smiling.

"Yeah." Gina grinned. "That's right."

Lily walked home quickly, hoping Mrs. Hiller would be up for another trip to Pet Palace. The sky overhead was turning dark and the wind had picked up. Dry leaves scuttled along the sidewalk like empty crab shells. But when she walked into the apartment, Mrs. Hiller was stretched out on the couch. A small cloth, neatly folded, was draped across her forehead.

"Hello, dear," she called, waving from the couch. "How was your day?"

"Okay," Lily said, dropping her knapsack inside the door. "Are you all right?"

"I just have a headache," Mrs. Hiller said. "Pick up your bag, dear."

"Oh." Lily grabbed her bag and sat down heavily on the couch. "Then I guess you don't want to go down to Pet Palace."

"Not today. I need to rest up for a little bit and then I'm going to make dinner." Mrs. Hiller glanced out the window. "Besides, it looks like it's getting ready to storm."

"Okay." Lily stood up and headed for the kitchen. She didn't want Mrs. Hiller to see how disappointed she was.

"I have a beautiful carrot and onion-dip platter out there, all ready for you!" Mrs. Hiller called.

Lily rolled her eyes as she glanced at the plate of carrots. Too bad Gina wasn't here, she thought. She'd probably eat the whole thing. She made a cup of coffee and then came back into the living room. "I'm gonna go downstairs and sit on the back porch," she said, walking quickly in case Mrs. Hiller stopped her to ask questions. "Just for a few minutes."

"All right, dear," Mrs. Hiller said. "Don't go anywhere else. I think that storm is moving in quickly." Lily closed the door tightly behind her, drowning out the clapping TV audience on *Dr. Phil.* "And be careful!" Mrs. Hiller called. "That fire escape is rickety!"

Lily descended the black metal steps slowly, holding on to the railing with one hand while balancing her coffee cup in the other. The steps were narrow and a few of them were loose, as if the screws underneath had fallen out. She liked to sit on the wide landing at the bottom of the steps and look at the skyline behind the trees.

The sky had gotten much darker by the time she arranged herself on the stoop, and the large trees in the distance were swaying in the wind. The air smelled like rain.

On her right was the back door to the apartment where the vampire neighbors had lived. She was glad they were gone. There hadn't been any more problems with noise since they'd left. A sharp gust of wind rattled the windows of the building. Lily put down her coffee mug and crossed her arms over her chest. Another burst of wind was followed by a low, whistling sound.

Suddenly, without warning, the vampire apartment door next to her blew open. Lily stared at it for a moment, frozen to the spot. Was someone behind it? It was open only halfway. She could hear her heart pounding in her ears. A sour taste pooled at the back of her tongue. She slid up the step behind her, feeling along with her hands.

The wind gusted again, slamming the door against the back wall. Now Lily could see partway inside. There were a few cardboard boxes sitting in the middle of an enormous empty space. She stood up on trembling legs and crept forward. The door was open completely, flat against the wall, so she knew there could not be anyone behind it. Was it possible that the empty apartment had mistakenly been left unlocked?

Placing her hand on the doorknob to steady herself, she took a few steps inside. The room was gigantic, even bigger than Mrs. Bing's classroom. Bare hardwood floors ran from one end of the room to the other, slick as a roller rink. She took a few more steps. A large mirror edged with gold petals sat on the mantel above a black marble fireplace. Lily ran her hand over the front of the fireplace. The marble was smooth and glossy. Two charred logs sat inside, crisscrossed over each other like an X.

Lily stood in front of the mirror and raised herself up on her tiptoes, but it was too high to see her reflection. The glass was dirty and smudged.

But the best part of the room was the enormous chandelier hanging from the ceiling. Lily had never seen anything like it. Shaped like an igloo, it had arms of gold and glass that draped and shivered above her. The opaque light from the windows at either end of the room shone through it, throwing diamond-shaped pockets of light against the walls. Lily stood against one of the walls and watched the little light shapes dance over her bare arms.

"Lily?"

Lily ran to the door as she heard Mrs. Hiller calling her upstairs.

"Lily? Are you all right?"

"Yes!" she yelled. "I'm okay! I'll be right up!"

"Just a few more minutes, dear. I don't want you outside when it starts to rain."

"Okay!"

She leaned against the outside wall of the empty apartment, listening until the door closed upstairs, and then walked back inside.

The room was filled with light and silence.

She lay down on the hardwood floor, just underneath the chandelier, and stared up at it.

It was her own Willowood.

9

EVERY DAY AFTER SCHOOL, LILY BEGGED Mrs. Hiller to take her back down to Pet Palace. Mrs. Hiller usually obliged, as long as Lily finished her homework first. Bernard was always there when they came, but he was usually with a customer. Mrs. Hiller had told Lily never to bother him when he was helping someone, so she tried to remember all the questions she had so she could ask him later.

There was so much she wanted to know! Like why did Beatrice have to be separated from Butch just because she was pregnant? Would Butch hurt her? Or did Beatrice just need her privacy? Mom had told Lily once that when she was pregnant, she had craved lemon ice and cheeseburgers all day long. Lily hadn't noticed any different foods in

Beatrice's cage yet, but wondered if she would start to have cravings later on. And what would her eggs look like once they were finally laid?

Every so often, Nate would come into the Reptile Room to say hello to Mrs. Hiller. He always gave her a hug, his furry red hat pulled down low over his eyebrows, and kissed her on the cheek. He said hello to Lily too, but only because Mrs. Hiller asked him to. A few times, Lily asked Nate about Beatrice, but he wasn't much help. He pushed out his bottom lip as he looked over at the yellow reptile sleeping under her heat lamp. "Who cares?" he said. "Lizards are so boring."

"Lily loves them," Mrs. Hiller replied. "She's into lizards the way you're into cats."

"Cats are smart," Nate said. "They understand people. Lizards are stupid."

"They are not!" Lily piped up finally. She was tired of all the mean things Nate said about lizards. It wasn't fair. She could say a million things about how horrible cats were, but she didn't. "Lizards are amazing. You just don't know what you're talking about."

Nate pushed out his bottom lip. "They're *stupid,*" he said. "I know more than you because I *work* here."

"Well, you don't work with the lizards." Lily kept going, despite the fact that Mrs. Hiller was poking her in the back. "So you can't say anything about them. Especially mean things. I prob'ly know more about them than you do, anyway."

Nate stuck out his bottom lip again. "Oh, yeah? If you know so much about lizards, then tell me what Boring Beatrice here is gonna do once she gets all her eggs out? *Huh?*"

"What do you mean?" Lily nervously glanced over in Beatrice's direction. "She's gonna wait for them to hatch. And then take care of them."

"Hah!" The long ends of Nate's red hat swung back and forth. He tilted his head back and laughed. "Ha *ha*! You don't know anything!"

"All right," Mrs. Hiller said. "Pipe down, the two of you. There's no reason to get all worked up about who knows what. You both know a great deal about your favorite animals. Let's leave it at that."

Lily ignored Mrs. Hiller. "What don't I know about the eggs?" Her voice was shaky.

Nate snapped the ends of his hat together. "You're the lizard expert. Figure it out."

"Nathaniel." Mrs. Hiller's voice was calm but firm. "Please. Stop."

Nate looked away from Lily and cleared his throat. He shrugged. "I don't really care, anyway. I have to get back to work." He waved. "Bye, Mrs. Hiller. See you soon."

"Good-bye, dear."

Lily ignored the fact that Nate didn't say good-bye to her.

She didn't want to say good-bye to him either.

Wednesday was Library Day for Mrs. Bing's class. They went only once a month. On their first visit, they'd had to stand around and look interested as the librarian, Mr. Barno, went on and on about the Dewey decimal system, which was on the computer now, and how to find books. This time, with the Dewey decimal system lecture out of the way, everyone was going to have twenty minutes to look for and pick out a book to read. After they finished reading, they had to write a book report.

Lily stood in line, hopping from one foot to the other, as Mrs. Bing yammered on about her instructions. Gina stood next to her quietly, with her hands folded. Lily wished Mrs. Bing would stop talking. Who cared about some dumb book report? She just needed to get over to the science section so that she could find a book about lizards.

"Okay, fifth graders!" Mrs. Bing clapped her hands. "Go find your books, please. And remember you are in a library. Whispers only!"

Gina turned, facing Lily. "What are you . . ."

Lily didn't wait to hear the rest of Gina's sentence. She ran toward the part of the library marked LIFE & SCIENCES and began looking up and down the shelf. Her heart began to race as she dragged her finger along the dusty book spines. In another minute, she would find out what Nate was talking about concerning Beatrice. What could he possibly know about her egg laying that could be so sinister sounding? Her finger stopped on a large book with the word "LIZARDS" on the side. She grabbed it.

"Lily?" Mrs. Bing was looking quizzically at her. "What are you doing in the Life & Sciences section?"

Lily glanced at the row of books next to her. With its gaps and spaces, it looked like a mouth with missing teeth. "Uh . . . finding a book for my book report." She held up the lizard book. "I'm going to do one on lizards. They're my favorite animals."

"Hmmm," Mrs. Bing said. Her eyes started to blink. "You haven't been listening very closely, have you?"

"To what?"

"To *me*." Mrs. Bing sounded annoyed. "Or to my instructions. I've told you at least three times that we are reading fiction. Made-up stories. Not nonfiction about animals, Lily."

"But . . ."

"Put that book back, please." Mrs. Bing pursed her lips.

Lily slowly slid the book into the empty spot.

"Thank you," Mrs. Bing said. "Now please join the rest of the class over in the Fiction section." Lily hesitated. "*Now*, Lily."

She ran.

10

BERNARD WAS BEHIND THE FRONT counter talking to a customer when Lily and Mrs. Hiller came into the store the next day. Duke was on Bernard's shoulder, chewing on a pecan. He was wearing an orange sweater with a yellow stripe around the middle. Bernard waved and held up a finger, indicating that he would be with them in a moment. Nate was nowhere to be seen.

Lily strolled into the Reptile Room and headed over to Butch and Beatrice's cage, as usual. Butch was sitting on a rock, eating some sort of leaf. But Beatrice was nowhere in sight. "Where's Beatrice?" she asked, running up one aisle and then down another. "Where'd she go? Where'd he put her? Did she lay her eggs? Was it time?"

Mrs. Hiller scratched her forehead. "Calm down, dear.

I'm sure Bernard will know. He'll be here in a minute."

Lily walked around nervously, nibbling a strand of hair. Not even the leopard-spotted geckos, who for some reason seemed especially active today, could catch her attention. She couldn't imagine where Beatrice had gone. Had something horrible happened to her? Is that what Nate had been referring to? Did iguanas die after they laid their eggs?

"Hey, girls!"

Lily whirled around as she heard Bernard's voice. "Bernard!" She waved her hand as she ran toward him. "Where's Beatrice? What happened to her? Where'd she go?"

"Whoa!" Bernard caught Lily by the shoulders. "Hold on, Lizard Lady! Beatrice is fine. She's just nesting."

"Oh." She tried to remember what Bernard had said the other day about Beatrice nesting.

"She has her own place, then?" she asked.

Bernard lifted his chin, indicating a direction in the back of the store. "Come on," he said. "I'll show you."

He opened a door that Lily had never seen before at the back of the Reptile Room. It was a small closet, empty except for a large hut-type structure made out of plastic, which sat on the floor. A thick piece of packing tape ran around the width of it and there was a narrow, rectangular opening in the front. Bernard put his finger to his lips as

Lily peered in. "Don't make any loud noises," he whispered. "She's in there, preparing a nest for her eggs."

Lily squatted down so that she was eye level with the rectangular opening. It looked like a tiny door. If she moved her head to the right, she could see part of Beatrice's yellow body. It looked as though she was digging.

"Mother iguanas are very picky about where they lay their eggs," Bernard explained in a soft voice. "They need damp sand and a warm, quiet spot." He pointed to what looked like a thin mattress under the opening. "That's a heating pad under there. Keeps it nice and toasty for her."

"Is she digging a spot for them right now?" Lily whispered.

"She might be," said Bernard. "But I doubt it. Iguanas have been known to build and then destroy up to forty nests before they finally settle on one to put the eggs into. They're very particular animals."

Lily scooted forward a little more on her heels so that she could see inside the makeshift door. Beatrice was turned away from her, and her back legs were moving rapidly, spewing up sand behind her. "How long till she lays them?" she asked.

"Hey, Pop! Whaddya doin'?" Nate's voice made everyone jump. Even Duke stood up on Bernard's shoulder and screamed.

"Damn it, Nate!" Bernard hissed. "Keep your *voice* down!"

Nate's face fell at his father's harsh reprimand. Mrs. Hiller reached out and rubbed his shoulder. "Don't scold him, Bernard. He didn't know we were back here."

"Come on," Bernard said impatiently. He nudged Lily with his shoe until she moved out of the way, and then shut the closet door. "The last thing Beatrice needs right now is to listen to the four of us out here bickering. She's never gonna lay those eggs with that kind of stress around."

They headed back toward the middle of the Reptile Room. Out of the corner of her eye, Lily noticed that Nate's shoulders were slumped, even though Mrs. Hiller was still patting his back. "Actually," Bernard said, coming to a stop in front of the blue-tongued skinks. "I've been meaning to ask you something, Lily." He rubbed his big belly and then reached up to scratch Duke's. "What would you say if I asked you to start coming down here for a reason?"

Lily glanced at Mrs. Hiller, who smiled at her. "What do you mean?"

"I mean, how would you like to have a little part-time job here? Unofficially, of course. You're still a little young for real working hours. But what would you think of coming down after school a few days a week to help Nate and me out around the store?"

Nate looked up. His eyes narrowed.

Lily jumped up and down. "Are you serious? Really? For real?"

"Of course for real." Bernard chuckled. "What other way is there?"

Nate stepped forward. "I don't need any help, Pop," he said. "I'm doing okay. Really, I am."

"We could all use a little help," Bernard said, giving Nate a look that said the decision was not up for discussion. Nate made a grunting sound and pulled on the end of his hat.

"She'll need to get permission from her mother first," Mrs. Hiller said, putting a hand on Lily's head.

"Of course!" Bernard nodded. "That goes without saying."

"She'll prob'ly say no," Nate said.

"Betcha she won't," Lily replied indignantly.

"Betcha she will." Nate's upper lip curled.

"Nate!" Bernard's voice came out like a bark. "Knock it off! It's time for you to get back to work!"

Nate bit the inside of his cheek. Lily kept her eyes on him as he slumped toward the door.

Then, just before he disappeared, he turned around and stuck out his tongue at her.

11

"PUH-LEEEAASE?" LILY'S FACE WAS PRESSED against the white wood of the bathroom door. "Please, Mom? Pleeeaase?" She could smell Mom's favorite vanilla and tangerine candle burning, which meant that Mom was soaking in the tub, which meant that she wanted to be left alone. Mom sometimes did this if she'd had a really long day. Once, after she worked three shifts in a row, Mom had gotten in the tub as soon as she got home and had fallen asleep. By the time she got out, her candle had burned down to a flat stub and her fingers were so wrinkled they looked like little white prunes.

Now her mother's voice drifted out from the other side of the door. "Lily. Please. Just give me five minutes, honey, okay?"

Lily slid down to the floor, resting her back along the bathroom door. She could see Weemis from where she sat, running up and down his plastic tree branch. Weemis had a tendency to get really active at night. Sometimes Lily could even hear him rustling around in a little pile of sand when she was trying to go to sleep, but she didn't mind. She wondered if Beatrice was still digging her nest.

"Okay, so let me get this straight," Mom said. Lily sat up straight and pressed her ear to the door. "You've just started a new school, and you're still trying to get adjusted to your new teacher and all the homework she gives, and you want to work at a pet store too. Mrs. Hiller told me . . ." Her voice was muffled.

"I can't hear you," Lily said, opening the door. The shower curtain was closed, but she could smell the cigarette smoke immediately. There was a splash of water as Mom jumped.

"You're smoking!" Lily said. "*Inside!*" She furiously yanked open the shower curtain.

Mom slid down into the water so that the suds came up to her neck. "I was not."

"You were too!"

Mom sank down deeper, nuzzling the suds with her chin. She lifted her right hand out of the water and dropped a soggy cigarette onto the ledge of the tub. "Okay, I was.

I had a terrible day and I'm exhausted and I come home and you start jumping all over me and . . ." She stopped, pressing her fingers against her lips, and closed her eyes. There was a long pause. "I'm sorry, honey. I didn't mean that. I'm just . . . so tired."

Lily sank down against the side of the tub as her mother tilted her head, resting it against the blue tile. "But smoking doesn't help anything." Lilly's voice was soft. "It just makes it worse, Mom."

Mom's eyes fluttered open. She stared up at the ceiling and then sat up a little. The skin on her face was damp and flushed. "You're right." She reached out and drew the backs of her knuckles along Lily's cheek. "You're absolutely, one hundred percent right."

"Promise me you'll try harder," Lily said.

Mom nodded. "I promise." She pushed the damp hair off her forehead. "Now, let's talk about this situation of yours."

Lily crossed her legs and sat next to the tub.

"What I was saying," Mom continued, "is that I'm just not sure you'll have enough time to do all your homework, plus work at the pet store. Mrs. Hiller told me yesterday that you've been having trouble with the essays your teacher has been giving you. I don't want you to fall behind."

"Well, I've already thought about all that," Lily said, thinking fast.

"Oh?" Mom asked.

"Yeah, I mean, I've already worked out how much time I'm gonna need to finish my homework every night, which is about an hour. And on nights that I have an essay due the next day, I wouldn't go at all. Bernard said it would be fine." Lily hadn't actually *talked* to Bernard yet about this, but she was pretty sure he would be okay with it.

Mom wasn't answering.

"Mom?" Lily asked. "Did you hear me?"

"Yeah," Mom said slowly. "I heard you. You figured that out all by yourself?"

Lily smiled.

She was in.

"Well, yeah. I'm not a *ba*by, you know."

"Wow," Mom said. "I'm impressed."

"So is that a yes?"

"Let me ask you something," Mom said.

Lily held her breath. She was *this* close. "What?"

"Do you like it here?" Lily didn't say anything. "I know it's been hard," Mom went on. "It's a big adjustment. But do you like your new school?"

"It's okay." Lily thought about telling Mom about Amanda, but then she changed her mind. Mom got all worked up about things like bullying. She'd go right into the principal's office and tell him about Amanda, and then Amanda would probably get into trouble. And then Lily's life would *really* be miserable. She decided to talk about Bailey instead.

"Bailey's getting all weird on me."

"What do you mean?"

Lily shrugged. "I call her all the time, but she's never around."

"Why not?"

"Oh, she's doing other things now, I guess. Her mom said she's joined soccer."

"*Soccer?* Since when has Bailey Sewell liked sports?"

"That's what I said." Lily started to pick her toenails. "The last time I called, she was home, but she was acting so weird. It's like she's turned into a different person."

"Hmmm," Mom said. "Well, have you made any friends at your new school yet?"

Lily shrugged. "There's one girl named Gina. She sits in front of me in class and sometimes I eat lunch with her. She's nice, but she's sort of nerdy."

"Oh, nerds can be fun," Mom said.

"That's 'cause *you're* a nerd."

Mom giggled. Then she got a serious look on her face. "You've got to give people a chance, honey. Even if they do seem like someone you would never get along with. People are always much more than what they seem."

"Yeah," Lily said, careful not to show her impatience. Mom loved to talk like this. "I know. You're right."

Mom looked at Lily out of the corner of her eye. "I'm serious, honey."

"I know!" she said again, ripping off a corner of her toenail.

"Stop that," Mom said. "The nail clippers are in the medicine cabinet."

Lily sighed. "So can I work at Pet Palace?"

"I think it'll be okay," Mom said. Lily let out a yelp and jumped to her feet. "Hold on!" Mom yelled. Lily sat back down. "We'll try it for two weeks and see how it goes, okay? If it's too hard with homework and everything else, you've got to tell Bernard that you can't stay with it. Agreed?"

"Agreed."

"Oh!" Mom said. "I forgot to tell you something."

"Yeah?"

"I talked to Aunt Wava today. She's coming up for a visit at the end of the month."

Lily stood up. "Really?"

Mom nodded. "She's a wreck, apparently, about her show. She said she needs to get away from the city for a few days and just relax."

"All right!" Lily pumped her fist in the air. "I can't wait! We haven't seen Aunt Wava in so long."

Mom smiled. "It's good to see you excited again, Lil."

Lily leaned down and buried her nose in her mother's hair. "Thanks for letting me do the pet store thing," she said. She drew back again. "Phew. You smell like smoke."

Mom lowered her hand and flicked a splash of water at her.

12

DURING HOMEROOM THE NEXT DAY, Amanda Peterson handed out her birthday party invitations. She made a big show of it, reading aloud the name on each envelope and then walking over and putting it on the person's desk. Every single person in the room, except Gina and Lily, got an invitation. Even Jonathan and Clive got invitations. Lily watched out of the corner of her eye as Clive opened his, made a weird noise with his lips, and shoved it across his desk. She stared at the fancy piece of white paper with gold scrolls around the edges. A slip of pale pink tissue lay atop the white paper, and beneath it, like so many starfish in a net, clung tiny pieces of gold confetti. Amanda's name was splayed across the top of the white paper in large cursive letters:

Amanda Gertrude Peterson

Gertrude?

Beneath Amanda's name were the details of the party:

Saturday, October 24
5:00–7:30 p.m.
The Zone Dance Factory
Wear your funkiest dance clothes!!
Prizes awarded to the best dancer!!
P.S. Amanda likes anything Hello Kitty and all kinds of lip gloss.

Lily sat back in her seat, hurt and relieved at the same time. She thought about Ms. Spicker, her third-grade teacher at Glenview, who had a rule about birthday invitations: If the whole class couldn't be invited to a party, then no invitations could be distributed at all. That way, she said, no one would be left out, and there would be no hurt feelings. At the time, Lily hadn't really given much thought to Ms. Spicker's rule, since she'd been invited to a lot of birthday parties. Now, however, she knew exactly why her teacher had done it.

"Jennifer?" Amanda called out, waving another envelope. Jennifer Triptle sat in the same row as Gina and Lily. Every day she wore an oxford shirt in a different color, buttoned all the way up to her chin, khaki pants, and a little blue belt with green turtles on it. Her clothes were pressed so sharply that you could see the creases from the back of the room. Jonathan and Clive called her "Miss Priss" behind her back.

"She's inviting *Jennifer*?" Lily whispered to Gina. "She'll never go. They don't even talk." Gina didn't say anything. Lily leaned in closer. "Did you see what Amanda's middle name is?" Gina mumbled something and then moved forward in her seat, away from Lily.

"What did you say?" Amanda's voice shot out behind Lily, like a slap. Lily hadn't realized she was so close. "What did you say about my name?" Amanda repeated.

Lily played dumb, holding out her hands and shaking her head from side to side. "Nothing," she answered. "I didn't say anything."

"You did too," Amanda said. The rest of the class was looking at her. "I heard you."

"I did not," Lily looked over helplessly as Mrs. Bing collected the pile of papers in front of her and tapped them into place. Her Styrofoam cup of coffee next to the papers already had red lipstick marks along the side.

"In your seats, please," Mrs. Bing said in a singsong voice. "It's almost time for the Pledge of Allegiance." Lily could feel Amanda's eyes on her as she sat back in her seat, but she stared straight ahead at Gina's glossy French braid. Gina turned her head and whispered out of the side of her mouth.

"What are you *doing*?"

Lily leaned forward a little. "What do you mean?"

"I mean, why do you even *care*?" Gina was whispering fiercely.

"I don't care," Lily replied. "I was just *say*ing."

"You're just making things worse," Gina said. "For both of us."

It was weird, Lily thought later, on the bus ride home, how a lot of people she met shied away from confrontation. She thought again about the situation with Bailey and Trisha Wheatley. She'd never thought of Bailey as a scaredy-cat. But when she thought about it some more, she realized that Bailey had done whatever it took to avoid Trisha Wheatley, even convincing Lily not to go up for more milk at lunch just so she wouldn't attract attention to herself. And now Gina was begging her not to tangle with Amanda. It wasn't like Lily was going to get into a fistfight with her, or hurt her in any way. Lily had never hit anyone in her life and she didn't want to start now. But there was something about letting a bully like Amanda get away with treating her the way she did that was starting to make her blood boil. There had to be some other way to stand up for herself that didn't involve getting physical.

There just had to.

13

AFTER SCHOOL, MRS. HILLER AND LILY walked down to Pet Palace.

Actually, Mrs. Hiller walked.

Lily ran.

It was her first day as a Pet Palace employee and she was breathless with excitement. Mrs. Hiller gave her a hug and told her she'd be back in three hours to walk her home. Bernard handed Lily a white apron to wear over her clothes. She stood still while he tied it in big loops in the back. "You have to put this on first thing whenever you come down to work," he said. "Otherwise you'll get too dirty."

"Did Beatrice lay her eggs yet?" Lily asked.

Bernard shook his head. "Not yet. But I'd bet money

she's gonna do it over the weekend." He led Lily over to the back of the store and pointed to a white door. "Nate's out back, washing the mice cages. I told him you were coming over to help."

Lily didn't move.

"You thinking twice about the deal?" Bernard asked.

"No." Lily swallowed hard and opened the door.

"Go ahead, then." Bernard chuckled. "Nate's got a big mouth on him, but he won't bite."

The backyard was small, just big enough for maybe four or five people to sit outside in lawn chairs and lie in the sun. There was a gated wooden fence around the perimeter and a single lilac bush in the far corner, which hung over, limp and exhausted looking. The grass, which was the color of Weemis, needed to be cut.

Nate was off to one side, kneeling over a metal cage and scrubbing it with a yellow sponge. His red fur hat was snapped tightly under his chin. He didn't look up.

"Hi," Lily said.

Nate frowned. "Are you ready to help?"

"Yup."

He staggered to his feet. The laces of his black and white sneakers were tied with enormous loops. "Okay, but *I'm* in charge. Pop even said. So you have to listen to me. Got it?" Lily nodded and pushed up her sleeves. Nate dipped his hand into a black bucket full of soapy water and pulled out another sponge. "You can do the gerbil cages." He pointed across the yard with a thick finger. "Over there." Lily looked over at a pile of small cages under the lilac bush. Even from this distance, she could see the dried brown crud that coated the metal bars.

"You have to take the bottoms of the cages out first," Nate said. "Do you know how?" Lily shook her head. Nate rolled his eyes dramatically. The front of his shirt was soaking wet and his blue jeans were covered with mud.

"How come you're not wearing an apron?" Lily asked, following him across the yard.

"Aprons are for sissies," Nate said. "Besides, I never get dirty." He motioned impatiently with his hand for Lily to come closer. "C'mere, I'll show you how to do it." Lily knelt down next to him and watched as he took apart one of the cages. The plastic bottom came off easily as Nate pushed a tiny button on the side. "See? This part pops out and then you lift the whole thing off." He glanced critically at Lily. "Do you think you can do it?"

She shrugged. "I'll try."

Nate locked the cage back into place again, stood up, and crossed his arms. The pressure was on. Lily reached around until she found the little button. When she pressed it, she felt the whole cage give, like a spring releasing. The wire part came off easily. She set it on the ground and grinned.

"Hmpf," Nate said, turning around. "Now you gotta wash it." He spread his hand out wide. "All of 'em. You gotta wash all of 'em."

There was nothing left for Lily to do except dip her sponge back inside the bucket and get started. But no matter how hard she scrubbed, it didn't look like anything was happening. The gerbil crud was stuck on tight, like glue. She soaped up her sponge again and rubbed again—even harder. Nothing.

"You gotta put some elbow grease into it!" Nate hollered behind her. "C'mon! *Scrub!*" Lily took a deep breath, focused on one tiny spoke in the cage, and tried again. "You're gonna have to work faster than that, Lily! There's eight of them cages!"

Lily stood up and plopped the sponge into the bucket. Water splashed out, soaking the cuffs of her new jeans, infuriating her even more. She put her hands on her hips and leaned forward. "Listen, I know you're in charge and everything—"

Nate cut her off, thrusting his chin forward. "Pop *said.* He did."

"*Fine.* I get it. You're in charge. But do you have to be so mean while you're in charge?"

Nate looked confused. "Mean?"

"Yeah. *Mean*. You've done nothing but be rude from the first day I met you. And I don't know why. I'm trying to be nice and all, but it's like you don't even notice."

"I'm not mean," Nate said softly. He stared down at the grass for a moment. "Lex Luthor is mean!" he said. His eyes were very wide.

"Lex Luthor?" Lily repeated.

"Yeah!" Nate unsnapped the sides of his hat excitedly. "He's Superman's biggest enemy. He's always trying to kill him! With Kryptonite! He's like the meanest guy in the world!"

Lily sighed. "Yeah, well. I don't really know much about Superman."

Nate looked confused again. "How come? Superheroes are the best!"

"I don't know. I just never got into any of that stuff."

"Even Wonder Woman?" Nate sounded so aghast that Lily almost laughed.

"Nope."

"You're missin' out, Lily." Nate stabbed his index finger in Lily's direction. "I'm telling you. You are *really* missing out."

Just then Bernard poked his head out the door. Duke was on his shoulder, nibbling on a Ritz cracker. He was wearing an orange sweater today with blue trim around the bottom and the sleeves.

"How's it going out here?" he asked. His voice was loud.

Nate jumped and dropped his sponge. "Real good, Pop," he said, looking over at Lily. "She's doing good."

Bernard gave Lily a wink. "Don't you let him distract you, Lily." He nodded toward Nate. "That one's a yapper. Talk your ear off, if you let him."

Nate drew his eyebrows together and pushed out his bottom lip. "I am not a yapper."

"Oh, you're a yapper, all right," Bernard said. He tapped the side of the door lightly. "Sometimes I wonder if you're gonna pull a muscle in that tongue of yours."

"Hrmpf," Nate said. He turned back around and stared at his bucket of water.

"I'll check back with you two in a little while," Bernard said. "You're doing great work, Lily. Keep it up, doll."

Lily grinned.

"I am *not* a yapper," Nate muttered to himself as the door shut behind his father. "I'm *not*." He looked over at Lily. "Do you go to school?"

Lily started in on the cages again. "Yup."

"What grade are you in?"

"Fifth."

"Oh, *fifth*," Nate repeated to himself, as if he knew

someone in fifth grade. "Where do you live?"

"Ivy Street." Lily pointed over Nate's shoulder with one free hand. "Just over that way, around the corner."

"Mrs. Hiller lives on Ivy Street," Nate said.

"Actually, she lives in the same building as me. She watches me after school."

Nate looked at Lily curiously for a minute. "How come your mom doesn't watch you?"

"She works."

"What about your dad?"

"I've never met my dad," Lily said, hoping he didn't ask her why.

"Why?"

"I just haven't. My mom said he left right after I was born."

"Why would he leave?" Nate asked. "Especially right after you were born? That's so dumb."

Lily shrugged impatiently. "I don't know. Like I said, I've never met him, so I've never gotten a chance to ask him."

The only sound was the sploosh of water as Lily dipped her sponge back into the bucket.

"That's what Beatrice is gonna do," Nate said after a few minutes.

Lily stopped scrubbing. "What do you mean?"

"She'll leave her eggs. Right after she lays them."

"What do you mean?" Lily stood up. "Where does she go?"

Nate shrugged. "She goes back in her cage with Butch and keeps on living her dumb, boring life."

Lily's heart was pounding. "Why?"

Nate shook his head. "I told you. Lizards are dumb. And stupid."

Lily stood rooted to the spot, trying to comprehend what Nate had just said. "Are you telling me the truth?" she asked finally. "Or are you just being mean again?"

Nate tossed a clean cage across the yard. It landed with a thump on the grass. "I'm telling you the truth. Me and Pop've been doin' this for a long time. Beatrice does the same thing every year. All iguanas do. Even the wild ones. Ask Pop."

"But if she doesn't take care of them, how do the babies survive?"

Nate threw another cage across the yard. "The ones in the wild have to figure it out for themselves, I guess. Ours don't have to worry about it." He paused. "We kill 'em."

Lily felt her knees buckle. "You *what*?" She steadied herself against the edge of the bucket.

"Whaddya think, we want five million baby iguanas running around this place?" Nate asked. "Every time

Beatrice lays, she puts out forty eggs. We used to keep a few, but nobody ever bought 'em. People don't know how to take care of baby iguanas, I guess. So now we just get rid of all of 'em. If we kept 'em all, this place'd be a zoo." He scowled. "This is a pet store here, not some stupid zoo."

Lily shook her head and sat down hard on the ground. "That's the most horrible thing I've ever heard in my entire life."

Nate pointed to her pile of cages. "You're falling way behind," he said. "And I'm not doin' those for you."

"How can you not even care?" Lily cried. "How could you kill a baby lizard?"

Nate scowled again. "They don't get to *be* lizards. We just take the eggs after Beatrice lays them and boil them. Then we dump 'em in the garbage. It's not a big deal. Really."

Lily tilted her head back, hoping that the whooshing sound in her ears would stop. She thought she might cry, but nothing came. She wondered what Nate would do if she started screaming. Instead, she dumped her sponge in the bucket. It disappeared beneath the water and then bobbed back up to the surface.

"Hey! Where're you going?" Nate yelled. Lily started walking to the door, reaching around her back to untie the apron. "You got six more cages, Lily! Get back here! I'm not doin' 'em!"

His voice faded behind the door as she opened and then shut it behind her. She thought she heard Bernard's voice as she walked through the store and placed her apron on the front counter, but she couldn't be sure.

There was only one thing she was sure of.

She was never coming back.

14

MRS. HILLER WAS NOT HAPPY TO SEE Lily walk through the front door.

"How did you get home?" she asked.

Lily shrugged. "I walked."

"You *walked? Alone?*"

Lily nodded. She realized suddenly that she hadn't looked at a single thing on her walk back through the center of the city. No store windows, no coffee shops, not even the waterfall. The only thing she could remember seeing was the sidewalk. And her shoes.

Mrs. Hiller put down her knitting. She was working on a new sweater for her grandson. "This is not going to work, Lily Sinclair, if you don't follow my instructions. You're not living in the country anymore. This is a city. Now, I promised your mother that I would walk you to and from the store every day. If you can't . . ."

"You don't have to worry about it," Lily said, plopping down on the couch. "I'm not going back."

Mrs. Hiller sat up straighter. "Why not?"

"I don't want to talk about it."

"Did something happen?"

Lily stared straight ahead.

"Did Bernard say something?" Mrs. Hiller pressed.

Lily shook her head.

"Nate?"

Lily shrugged. "Yeah. But not the way you're thinking. It wasn't his fault." She got up. "I'm gonna go lie down."

The inside of her room was cool and dark. Mrs. Hiller always pulled the shades down for some reason. Usually, Lily yanked them back up, but today, she walked directly over to Weemis's cage and lifted him out of it. He scuttled up and down her hand for a minute, a little alarmed at having been removed so abruptly from his cage, but Lily bent her face down close to him and whispered in his ear.

"It's just me, little guy. It's just me. I just wanted to tell you how much I love you." She stuck out her little finger and smiled as Weemis wrapped his tiny tail around it. She didn't know how or even when he had learned how to do that, but the gesture always made her incredibly happy.

"I just love you so much, little guy, and I want you to know that I will never let anything bad happen to you." Lily brought her hand up so that Weemis was at eye level. He blinked once, and then again. "I promise."

She stretched out on her bed, placing Weemis on her thigh. Watching him scurry up and down the length of her jeans, she tried to sort out the information still swirling around in her head. She didn't know which bit of information hurt more: the fact that Beatrice wanted nothing to do with her babies after the eggs were laid, or that Bernard and Nate killed them because they couldn't keep them. She pushed the crook of her elbow over her eyes and pressed down hard to stop the tears from coming. After a while she settled back, arranging herself against her pillow. A corner of her father's picture inside her pillowcase poked into her back. She reached inside, grabbed the picture, and threw it across the room.

The next day was Saturday. Lily slept in late and then lay in bed even longer, playing with Weemis. She let him crawl up and down her fingers and into the crevices between them. Sometimes he would stop, balancing himself on the tip of her thumb, and then look around. She placed a little white mealworm in the middle of her other hand, and nudged him toward it, but he didn't seem interested.

"It's okay," Lily said, putting Weemis back in his cage. "You don't have to eat it." She fastened the screen top shut and got back under the covers. She squeezed her eyes shut, trying not to think of Beatrice or her poor little eggs.

There was a knock on her door. Lily poked her head out from under the covers. "Come in!"

Mom opened the door, carrying a big tray. In the middle of it was Lily's favorite mug, filled with coffee, and a plate stacked with three pieces of peanut butter toast. "Hi, honey. I thought you might like some breakfast in bed."

Lily scooted over so that Mom could sit down next to her. She stretched her legs out flat as Mom arranged the tray on top of them. "What's this?"

Mom smoothed a piece of hair behind her ear. "I thought you might be hungry. Mrs. Hiller told me you fell asleep last night without eating dinner."

Lily slurped her coffee. "Yeah, I wasn't that hungry."

"Anything else going on?" Mom asked.

Lily shook her head. She fiddled with the crust on one of her pieces of toast. Mom had left it in too long. It was dark and crispy. "I miss you," Lily said suddenly.

Mom's eyes got big. "What do you mean, sweetie? I'm right here."

Lily pinched part of the crust off with her fingernail. It splintered into a fine black powder. "Ever since we moved, it's like I never see you anymore. You have to work late all the time and . . ."

"Honey, that's so I can make more money." Mom looked worried. "Our rent is higher now and I wouldn't be able to afford a lot of things if I wasn't working those extra hours."

Lily pressed her fingertip against some of the toast powder and licked it off. "I know."

"Have you talked to Bailey again?" Mom asked. "Is she being any nicer?"

"No."

"No, you didn't talk to her, or no, she's not being any nicer?"

"No, I didn't talk to her."

"Why?" Mom reached out and touched Lily's chin with her fingers. "Did you guys get into a fight?" Two tears slid down Lily's face and plopped onto the toast. "Oh, *honey*!" Mom said, getting up and taking the tray off Lily's legs. She sat back down again and cradled Lily in her arms. "What happened?"

Lily climbed into Mom's lap. It was exactly the place she wanted to be. She told her more about the last conversation she'd had with Bailey, how she'd been replaced by Trisha Wheatley, and how sad she felt wondering if she was Bailey's friend any longer.

Mom hugged her tightly. "Oh, sweetie," she said. "Sometimes it's the people we love that hurt us the most. I'm sure Bailey will come around if you give her some time."

Lily wiped her face and buried her head against Mom's shoulder. "Maybe."

They sat there for a few moments without saying anything.

"How about your first day at the pet store?" Mom stroked Lily's hair gently. "What was that like?"

"Horrible."

Mom drew back. "Why? What happened?"

"They kill baby iguanas, Mom!"

Mom's eyebrows skittered together over her blue eyes. "What? Why would they do that?"

"'Cause they don't want them! That's what Nate told me." Lily took a deep breath. "Right now, probably at this very moment, Beatrice is in her nest, laying about forty eggs. And when she's done, she'll crawl out of her nest, go back with Butch, and Nate and Bernard will take all the eggs and put them in a pot of boiling water."

Mom made a little gasping sound. She kept stroking Lily's hair. "Well, honey, I guess they can't keep them all. Or maybe they can't sell them. You know, maybe that's just what they have to do."

Lily stared down at a fold in her comforter. "It's

horrible." She paused. "And I'm not going back."

"Oh, honey. I don't know if you have to take such a drastic step."

"I can't work there knowing that they kill lizards!" Lily reached over and put her hand on the side of Weemis's cage. "I love lizards," she said softly.

"I know you do." Mom squeezed her hard. "And I love that you love lizards enough to stick up for them. You do what you think is right. That's what counts. I'm proud of you either way."

Lily hugged her. "Thanks, Mom," she said. "It means a lot to me."

"*You* mean a lot to me," Mom said. "The most."

15

ON MONDAY, AS LILY GOT ONTO THE bus and headed down the aisle, Amanda stuck out her foot and tripped her. Everyone laughed as she fell, grabbing the sides of the seats as her feet flew out from under her. Lily's math book catapulted out of her arms and slid under Amanda's seat. Quick as a flash, Amanda grabbed it and held it over her head.

"C'mon, Amanda," Lily said, pushing the hair out of her face. "Just give it to me." She could feel something growing inside of her, like a balloon inflating. If it popped, she wasn't sure what would happen next.

"Not until you apologize for making fun of my middle name," Amanda said. The kids around her were watching to see what Lily would do. "It's my great-grandmother's name, you know."

"Sorry," Lily said.

"Yeah, right," Amanda said, tossing her head. "Like you even mean it." She glanced at Lily's sneakers. "Do you know you look like an idiot with those orange shoelaces? Like some kind of clown." Two of the girls behind her laughed out loud. Amanda turned to them. "I mean, who *wears* stuff like that, right?"

The girls stopped laughing suddenly. They were looking at something behind Lily. Amanda turned back around. Her mouth fell open a little. Lily felt a hand on her shoulder. It was the Freakazoid. With all the distraction around her, Lily hadn't even felt the bus come to a stop.

"What's going on here?" The Freakazoid was staring at Lily's math book in Amanda's hand. Her earphones dangled around her neck.

Amanda held out the book to Lily. "Nothing," she said. "She dropped her book and I was just giving it back to her." Lily took the book and pushed it into her backpack.

The Freakazoid scratched the tip of her nose. "You keep your feet under the seats," she said, pointing at Amanda with her index finger. "Or you can walk to school tomorrow, you got it?" Amanda tilted her head, licked her lips, and nodded her head the merest bit. Her cheeks were pink.

The Freakazoid looked at Lily. "You okay?" Lily nodded. "Find a seat, then," she said. "I'm running late." Lily hurried to her seat in the back and held her backpack on her lap. Amanda stayed put for the rest of the ride, talking in whispers to the girls around her. Gina's stop was next. She kept her eyes on the floor and scooted into the front seat, where she always sat.

Lily stared out the window, turning once to glance at the front of the bus. The Freakazoid was swiveling her head in circles to the music pounding in her ears.

For a moment, Lily wondered what her real name was.

"What book did you end up picking for the book report again?" Gina was slurping some sort of cloudy-looking soup out of a green thermos.

"*Alice in Wonderland*," Lily answered. After Mrs. Bing demanded that Lily put back the book about lizards and find a fiction book, she had decided to select *Alice in Wonderland*. If Aunt Wava was going to take her to see the statue of Alice in Central Park, the least she could do was read the story.

"Oh, that's right," Gina said. "I forgot. Did you finish it?"

Lily shook her head. "I haven't even started. I thought it would be like the Disney movie, but it's not. The pictures are totally different. And it's so *long*."

"It's not that long." Gina shrugged. "It's got a great plot." She took another sip of soup. "And remember, you have the rest of the quarter to finish it."

"Yeah," Lily replied. She tried to remember what "plot" meant. "What is that you're eating?"

"Miso soup," Gina said, tipping the thermos back to empty the contents down her throat. She pronounced it "meeso." "My favorite."

"Your mom make it?" Lily didn't know why she asked this every day, since the answer was always yes, no matter what kind of dish—or thermos—Gina brought.

"Of course." Gina shoved her cookie across the table. "Peanut butter chocolate chip. You can have the whole thing, if you want. I'm already full."

"Wow." Lily slid the cookie over to her side. "Thanks."

Gina opened a plastic container filled with green leaves, slices of hard-boiled egg, and orange sections. She poured a small jar of cranberry-colored dressing over the top and then snapped the jar shut again. "Don't you get tired of eating the same thing every single day?" she asked, inserting a forkful of lettuce into her mouth.

"No," Lily said uncertainly. She took another bite of her sandwich. Today, for some reason, it tasted a little drier than usual. "I love peanut butter."

"I love a lot of things," Gina said. "But I don't eat them constantly. You gotta switch things up. Try something new."

"You sound like Mrs. Hiller," Lily said.

"Who's that?"

"This lady that watches me after school until my mom gets home from work. She's always trying to get me to eat fruits and vegetables and all this other weird stuff. It drives me nuts."

"Why?"

"Because I don't like it!" Lily said. "It's gross."

Gina seemed unfazed. "Have you ever tried any of it?"

"*No,*" Lily said. "But I know I would hate it."

"How do you know?" Gina pressed.

"I just do." Lily was starting to understand why Mom got so annoyed when she asked "Why" too many times. "And I don't want to talk about it anymore."

Gina shrugged. "Okay." She popped an orange section into her mouth and licked her lips. "But you'll never know unless you try."

16

MRS. HILLER FINISHED HER GRANDSON'S sweater and mailed it off to him. She was working on a hat and scarf set for her son, Benjamin, when Lily came in from school. There was a commercial on TV about the Oprah show, which would be on soon. It was about a lady who had survived a flood by hanging on to the top of the car for twenty-two hours. Lily didn't know if she could hang on to *anything* for twenty-two hours.

"Hey," she said, dropping her backpack and breathing on her hands. "It's getting cold out."

"I know," Mrs. Hiller said. "I'm going to make you a scarf as soon as I finish this one for Benjamin. Pick up your bag, dear." Lily brought her bag into the living room and sat down on the couch. Mrs. Hiller pointed to the little table in front of them. "I fixed your coffee. Tell me how your day was."

Lily looked at Mrs. Hiller in surprise. Sometimes Mrs. Hiller did things that really threw her for a loop. In a good way. "Thanks," she said, taking a slurp of coffee. Not bad. She took another sip. Mrs. Hiller picked up her pile of yarn and began moving her needles. The yarn was a dark purple color with specks of red in it.

"Where did you learn to knit?" Lily asked.

"My mother taught me," Mrs. Hiller said.

"Do you remember the first thing you ever made?"

Mrs. Hiller closed her eyes and tilted her head back on the couch. "I don't think I can remember that far back. But do you want to know what my favorite thing to make is?"

Lily nodded, figuring she'd say something like baby hats or socks. Instead, Mrs. Hiller leaned forward with a little smile on her face. "Duke's sweaters."

Lily's mouth dropped open. "*You* made all those little sweaters?"

Mrs. Hiller smiled and nodded. "When Bernard brought Duke home from South America, he was sick. He had a terrible chest cold and couldn't seem to get warm. He just shivered all the time, the poor thing. So I went home and made the smallest little sweater and pair of pants I ever made in my life. It took me about two hours. Bernard cried when he saw them."

"Why would he cry?" Lily asked. "I would think he'd be happy."

"Oh, he was, dear. He cried because he was so relieved. We got the sweater and pants on Duke and he curled right up next to Bernard's ear and went to sleep. Never shivered again." Mrs. Hiller smiled broadly.

"They're so adorable!" Lily was seriously impressed. "How many does he have now?"

Mrs. Hiller stopped knitting for a moment and thought. "I'd have to say about twenty."

Lily whistled through her teeth. "You're spoiling him."

"*Bernard* spoils him." Mrs. Hiller snorted. "He orders four or five sets every Christmas for that animal. He pays me good money too." Mrs. Hiller paused, looking sideways at Lily. "You think you'll reconsider working down at Pet Palace?"

Lily shook her head. "No."

"That's too bad," Mrs. Hiller said. "Bernard just thinks the world of you."

Lily stared down into her coffee. "Do you think Bernard is kind of mean to Nate?"

Mrs. Hiller's knitting needles paused for a moment and then started up again. "Bernard's a wonderful man," she said. "But he's got a temper. And it's only gotten worse since Marilyn died."

"Who's Marilyn?"

"His wife. Nate's mother. She and I were very close friends."

"She died?"

Mrs. Hiller nodded. "She had a weak heart. It was very sudden. She died in the ambulance on the way to the hospital."

"That's terrible." Lily tried to imagine what Nate's mother had looked like.

"Nate misses her a great deal," Mrs. Hiller said. "It's been five years since she died, but I'm sure it feels like yesterday to him. Those two were inseparable. You know, for the first eight years of his life, Nate didn't so much as let go of her hand. If she tried to walk out of the room without him, he would cry his eyes out."

"Because of . . . the way . . . he is?" Lily asked. "Being kind of . . . slow?"

"It's called Down syndrome, dear," Mrs. Hiller said. "That's how he was born. And that might have been part of it. But I think a bigger reason was because his mother didn't really encourage him to do things for himself. She was a lovely, wonderful woman, but she did everything for him. *Ev*erything."

"Bernard's not like that," Lily said.

Mrs. Hiller snorted. "Bernard has the patience of a gnat." Her voice softened. "And he's always been very hard on Nate. Even when Nate was little and they weren't sure yet what he could or couldn't do, Bernard pushed him."

"Why?" Lily asked.

Mrs. Hiller put down her knitting next to her on the couch. "I don't know really." She sighed. "Some people are just born impatient. And maybe Bernard just didn't want to accept the fact that he had been blessed with a mentally handicapped son. Maybe he thought if he pushed Nate, he would be able to overcome his disability in some way." She paused. "It's funny, though. As close as Nate was to his mother, he is very much his father's son. That boy's got a temper just like Bernard."

"He *can* be kind of rude," Lily agreed.

"Oh, yes," Mrs. Hiller said, nodding her head. "He even got impatient with his mother on occasion. She came over to my place a few times after they argued and talked to me about it. It was very upsetting to her." Mrs. Hiller sighed. "After she died, though, his temper got worse. He began to throw fits. Bernard even had to put him in a special home for a while because he would throw things and scream so loudly."

"What was he mad about?"

"Well, I'm sure he never understood why his mother left in an ambulance one night and then never came home again. And there are things that have to do with Down syndrome that none of us really understands yet. That poor boy is only thinking on the level of an eight- or nine-year-old."

"I'm eleven," Lily said. It seemed to her as though Nate was a lot younger than she was in some ways, even though he was thirty-six years old.

Mrs. Hiller nodded. "Exactly," she replied.

17

NOW THAT LILY HAD STOPPED GOING to Pet Palace in the afternoon, she spent most of her time downstairs in the empty apartment. She began to make it her own, sneaking the broom down from the kitchen when Mrs. Hiller wasn't looking and sweeping the hardwood floors. An old rag draped over the end of the broom made the perfect feather duster. She used it to poke out the soft cobwebs that had collected in the corners and to wipe off the thin film of dust on top of the fireplace. Next, she brought down her *Alice in Wonderland* postcard from Aunt Wava. She dragged one of the cardboard boxes underneath the chandelier, climbed up on the box, and tied the postcard to one of the dangling glass arms. A few of her throw pillows, arranged like little mushroom caps in front of the fireplace, served as chairs. Most days she would stretch out on the floor with her head on one of the pillows and stare up at the chandelier.

It was pretty cool.

And it was all hers.

But it would have been better if Bailey were there.

During gym Mr. Finkelsteiner announced that the dodgeball game was going to be divided into two semifinal rounds and then a final championship. The whole class would be divided into two teams, with the first team throwing the ball from the outside of the circle at the second team, who would be inside the circle. Then the teams would switch places. The last player from each team left standing inside the circle would then compete against the other in the championship round. The winner would be able to choose whatever he or she wanted to do for gym for the next two weeks.

The excitement in the air was palpable. Clive and Owen swung their arms around in their sockets and bounced on their toes from side to side. "You and me, O," said Clive. He punched at the air with his balled-up fists. "We'll take everybody out till it's just me and you."

Lily rolled her eyes. Boys always assumed they were going to win everything when it came to sports. It was so annoying. Still, she didn't really care who won. Leave it to Mr. Finkelsteiner to turn an already bloodthirsty sport into something even more cutthroat. She planned to get out as quickly as possible, so that she could stand safely on the outside of the circle and not have to worry about getting pummeled again.

Mr. Finkelsteiner selected the teams, counting off students randomly by even numbers. Gina, Lily, and Owen were on the same team. Amanda and Clive were on the opposite side. Thankfully, Lily and Gina's team was directed to the outside of the circle first, where they only had to throw. Amanda's team had excellent players. The round went on and on, as Lily's team struggled to get them out. Lily began to get tired as she stood there, watching the ball zoom back and forth, missing students' feet by half an inch over and over again. Amanda and Clive, who were obviously the two strongest players on the team, strolled casually around inside the circle, purposefully looking bored.

After a while, Mr. Finkelsteiner blew his whistle. "Everybody move in!" he yelled at Lily's team. "Let's make the circle smaller or we'll be here all night!"

That helped a little bit. With less space to move around in, Darren Tokash was taken out, along with Jennifer Triptle and Robert Gaudio. Now the only two left were

Amanda and Clive. The ball went around and around the circle, with the players from Lily's team struggling valiantly to clip Amanda's and Clive's heels. Gina threw one that missed Clive by less than an inch. The sound of screeching sneakers echoed throughout the gym, punctuated by shouts and groans as Amanda and Clive managed to dodge every ball.

Finally, Mr. Finkelsteiner blew his whistle again. "Two more steps in!" he said to Lily's team. "Let's tighten this circle up and get someone out. Class is almost over!"

Lily could see the excitement in Amanda's face as the other team began to close in around her. Clive was still hopping from side to side, shaking his arms out, but Amanda stayed perfectly still, watching the ball intently as it drifted from one player to another. She reminded Lily of a wolf, the way her eyes narrowed and the muscles in her legs tensed.

Darren Tokash aimed for Clive and threw the ball.

It missed.

Margaret Haggerson rolled the ball in an arc toward Amanda.

It missed.

Lily took the ball and tossed it between Amanda and Clive.

It missed.

Gina grabbed the ball and wound it up. Without taking her eyes off Amanda, she drew her arm back, cupping the ball like a baby, and let it rip.

It nailed Clive squarely on the heel.

Clive screamed and sank to the floor, burying his face in his hands.

Amanda leapt into the air, pounding an invisible object with both fists. "Yeah!" she bellowed. "Yeah! Yeah! Yeah!" Her group of friends rushed around her, jumping up and down and shrieking with joy. Across the gym, Clive crossed his arms and sulked.

Amanda was Championship Player Number One.

Next week, they would find out who would be Championship Player Number Two.

18

OCTOBER BLEW IN SUDDENLY WITH A sharp wind. The trees on Ivy Street began to turn gold and ruby and tangerine. The leaves drifted down around Lily like little pieces of stained glass as she made her way to the bus stop a few days later. The bus came early, before the sun had a chance to warm up everything, and as Lily stood there, waiting for it to lumber around the corner, the wind felt like a knife going through her ears. At least Mom let her wait for the bus by herself. Since it came right to the corner of their street, she hadn't insisted that Mrs. Hiller accompany her, the way she had for the walk down to Pet Palace. Thank goodness. Lily didn't know what she'd do if Mrs. Hiller had to stand next to her every morning in her blue pom-pom slippers.

She kicked a pile of new leaves and shoved her hands deep into her pockets. The wind blew again more sharply, stinging her face. She turned around so that she wasn't facing it.

"Lily!" She turned around and then did a double take.

It was Nate.

Nate? She hadn't seen or heard from him since she had walked out of Pet Palace. He was farther down the street in the opposite direction from where the bus was coming. His hands were in his pockets, and the sides of his red hat flapped open. His awkward gait was even more pronounced as he hurried toward her. She stepped back, a little alarmed. "Lily!" he called again. "C'mere! I gotta show you something!" There was a squeal of brakes behind her. Lily turned around. The bus was two blocks away.

"I can't," she said. "I have to go to school."

Nate rushed up to her all at once, almost knocking her over. His nose was running and his breath smelled like bacon and eggs. He drew his hands out of his pockets and shoved them toward Lily. "These are for you."

Lily took a step back. "What . . . what are they?"

Nate turned his hands over and then opened them slowly. "I could only get three of 'em. Pop wouldn't turn around long enough for me to get more."

Lily let her backpack drop to the sidewalk as she

stared at Beatrice's eggs. Behind her, the bus rumbled up another block. "Nate," she whispered. He placed the eggs gently in her hands. They were soft and leathery, not at all like the eggs Mom cracked in the morning for breakfast. "But why . . . why are you giving them to me? Why didn't you just keep them . . ."

Nate took a step back. "I don't *want* 'em. I think lizards are boring. And stupid." He paused. "But you don't."

Lily bit her lip. "But I'm going to school, Nate. I can't take them with me. And my mom would never, ever let me have these in our house."

"Don't you have a secret place?" Nate asked. "That you could put them in while you're at school? And so your mom wouldn't find out?"

Lily stared into Nate's face. The red fur on his hat made his eyes look even bluer. "A secret place?" she repeated.

Nate nodded his head vigorously. "Yeah!"

The bus pulled up in front of them, wheezing to a stop. Lily turned her head as the doors opened with a sucking sound. The Freakazoid bounced up and down in her seat, jerking her head under her earbuds. She raised her eyebrows as Lily stood there, not moving.

"Um," Lily said, taking a few steps away from the bus. "Yeah, I do have a place like that." She looked at the Freakazoid and shook her head. The Freakazoid shrugged, pulled the doors shut, and stepped on the gas. The bus roared down the street.

Lily turned to Nate. "But you gotta come with me. If I'm skipping school for these eggs, you gotta show me what to do with them."

"I don't have a lot of time," Nate said. "Pop thinks I'm at the grocer's. He's gonna be lookin' for me." He walked very close to Lily as she led the way back down the street, almost as if she weren't there. A few times, he practically knocked her off the sidewalk. Lily noticed a backpack on his shoulders that she hadn't seen earlier. She wondered if it was throwing him off.

"Okay." Lily moved over so she wouldn't fall into the street. "But you gotta show me what to do with these eggs before you go back. I don't know the first thing about hatching baby iguanas." She put her finger to her lips as they circled around her building. "Now, remember, Mrs. Hiller is right upstairs." She spoke in a whisper. "You have to be superquiet or we'll get in huge trouble."

Nate's eyes bloomed wide. "Okay!" he said excitedly.

But when Lily pushed open the door of the empty apartment, he let out a bellow. "Whoa! This place is—"

Lily clapped her hand over his mouth. "Shhhhh! I told you you have to be *quiet*!"

Nate drew his shoulders up around his ears. "Sorry." His lips moved behind Lily's hand. Lily withdrew it slowly. Nate looked around for a moment, taking everything in. He put his hands on his back and tilted his head when he looked up at the chandelier. "This place *rocks,*" he said finally. "How'd you find it?"

"These weird people used to live in it," Lily said. "And then they moved out. Someone must've forgotten to lock it, I guess, because one day I was down here, and the wind was blowing really hard and the door just flew open."

"Cool," Nate breathed. He shoved his hands in his pockets and shifted his attention to the pillows, where Lily was sitting. "Can I sit on one?"

Lily patted the blue one next to her. "Of course." She drew the eggs out of her pockets and studied them as Nate sat down noisily. "I still can't believe you brought these for me," she whispered. "It's so . . ." She shook her head. "I don't know. I never expected it."

"That's 'cause you think I'm mean," Nate said. He sat hunched over with his legs crossed. The little square of pillow vanished beneath him. "And I'm *not,*" he said, leaning forward. "Only Lex Luthor is mean. Okay?"

Lily nodded. "Okay." She looked down at the eggs again. "Do you really think they'll hatch?"

Nate nodded. "You gotta use the right stuff for them, though."

"Like what?"

He shrugged off his knapsack. "I got it in here. Pop and I hatched some eggs a few times, so I know what to do." Lily watched wordlessly as Nate unpacked three plastic Tupperware containers, a large bag of what looked like loose white dirt, a small shovel, two bottles of water, and a shoe box.

"You gotta do two things with the eggs," Nate said, tearing open the bag of dirt. "You gotta keep 'em clean and you gotta keep 'em warm." He poured some of the dirt mixture into one of the containers. It spilled all over the place. "This stuff is called vermiculite. I don't know what it is, but it's what Pop used. I think it helps the eggs breathe." He grunted as more spilled on the floor. "Or something like that."

Nate unscrewed a water bottle and poured a thin stream into each container of dirt. He stirred it with his finger, packed it down with the backs of his knuckles, and then pinched a little between his hands. "Too wet," he said, and added more dirt. This time, the dirt mixture got his approval when he pinched it. "Okay. Now we just gotta get it ready for the eggs." He scooped out a small hollow with his fingers, took an egg out of Lily's hand, and placed it inside the indentation. It sat almost level with the dirt around the edges. Nate pushed the dirt down from the sides and packed it against the egg, like a little blanket. Then he snapped the lid tightly on the container. He held up the whole thing and shoved it in Lily's lap. "That's how they hatch," he said. "You gotta keep these in a real warm place, and come down every day and open the lid for thirty minutes." He sat back on his haunches. "That's about it. Now, in about ninety days, if everything goes right, you should have three baby iguanas."

Lily had been quiet during Nate's demonstration, but now, when she tried to talk, nothing came out. She opened her mouth once more. Nothing.

Nate stared at her. Little beads of sweat had collected on his upper lip. "Lily?" He jabbed her gently in the shoulder. "You got it?" She nodded. He stood up. "I gotta go, then." She didn't move. He headed toward the door, fiddling with the silver snaps on his cap.

"Nate!" Lily stood up, still clutching the other two eggs in her hands. Nate turned around. He was wrestling with the snaps on his hat, still trying to close them.

"What?"

"Um . . . thanks," Lily said.

"Oh, yeah." The snaps clicked together under Nate's thick fingers. "It was no biggie." He lifted his hand as he walked toward the door. "See ya, Lily."

"See you," she whispered.

19

"WHERE WERE YOU YESTERDAY?" GINA asked as Lily walked to her desk the next morning. Gina's hair was twisted into two elaborate French braids, secured at the ends with small yellow bows. "Were you sick?"

Lily nodded. "Yeah. Kinda." She sat down and got her math book and pencil out of her desk.

"But you feel better now?" Gina asked.

"Yeah," Lily said. "I feel great."

She felt more than great, she realized. She felt better than she had in a long time, thanks to Willowood and her iguana eggs. After Nate had left, she had spent the better part of the morning trying to copy exactly what he had done, filling the other two containers, making sure the dirt wasn't too wet, and carving out small indentations for the eggs. They were all in the shoe box Nate had brought, with the lids tightly closed, hidden inside the fireplace. It was the warmest place in the apartment, away from the drafty windows and cold floors.

She'd stayed inside Willowood for the rest of the day, peeking outside only when she heard the afternoon school bus rumble by. Then she ran upstairs, flinging open the door and throwing her backpack to the floor. Mrs. Hiller was absorbed in yet another episode of *Dr. Phil*. She had not thought to check the messages on the answering machine, one of which had been left by the school's attendance office, and which Lily erased as soon as Mrs. Hiller went into the kitchen to get her snack. No one had suspected a thing.

"You didn't really miss much," Gina said, turning around in her seat. "It was kind of a slow day."

"Good," said Lily.

"You start *Alice in Wonderland* yet?"

Lily shook her head. "Nope."

"What were you doing with that weird guy yesterday?" Amanda suddenly appeared next to Lily's desk. Her lips were slick with strawberry lip gloss and she smelled like hairspray. "I saw you yesterday at the bus stop with him. He was talking to you and then you guys went off together." She put her hand on her hip.

The rest of the classroom had fallen silent. Everyone

was waiting for Lily to respond. Gina's eyes flitted worriedly from Amanda to Lily and then back again.

Lily took a deep breath and focused on one of Gina's yellow hair ribbons. She thought about how the Freakazoid had stopped Amanda in her tracks just by the tone of her voice. Of course, the Freakazoid was an adult. Amanda had to listen to her if she wanted to keep riding the bus. She cleared her throat. "It's none of your business," she said, making her voice as steady as possible.

"*What'd* you say?" Amanda leaned in so close that Lily could see the individual hairs in her eyebrows.

Lily reached under her desk and grabbed her knees to stop them from shaking. "I *said,* it's none of your business. Now leave me alone."

Mrs. Bing breezed in just then, carrying her Styrofoam cup of coffee and a stack of folders. "All right, everyone! Sit down, please. It's time for the Pledge of Allegiance."

Amanda leaned in an inch closer to Lily's face. Her breath was hot against Lily's ear. "You're done," she whispered. "You got it, Sinclair? *Done.*"

Lily removed the lids from the iguana egg containers and set them aside. Nate said the lids needed to be taken off every day for a half hour so that the eggs could breathe. She peeked inside each one, trying to tell if anything was happening, but nothing looked any different. Ninety days seemed like a lifetime, she thought as she stretched herself out on her pillows.

She tried not to think about Amanda as she lay there, but it was hard not to. Lily knew Amanda was one of those people who would play dirty if she had to. Just like Trisha Wheatley. Lily's standing up to her in class—in front of everyone, no less—was going to take Amanda a long time to forget. Had it been the right thing to do? Or had she just dug herself into an even deeper hole?

A soft tap on the back door jerked her to her feet. Tiptoeing over, she leaned into the doorjamb and put her ear against it. The tap sounded again, louder this time. "Hey, Lily! It's Nate!" Lily winced. His voice was much too loud. She swung open the door. "Hey!" he said. "Didn't you hear me? I was knock—"

She pulled him in and pressed her finger against his lips. "You have to be *quiet*, Nate! I already told you Mrs. Hiller is right upstairs! If she finds out we're down here, we're both gonna get in trouble. Now, listen, if you can't whisper when you come here, I'm not letting you in anymore."

He shrugged her off. "All *right*," he said morosely. "Fine." He strode into the big room and sat down on one of the pillows. "I only got like fifteen minutes anyway. I just came over to make sure you got the other two eggs set up right." He peered inside the shoe box, poking the containers and grunting.

"Whaddya think?" Lily asked. "Did I do all right?" She sat down next to him.

"They look okay." Nate stood up. "I don't like those pillows," he said. "They're too small for my butt." He got up and began to wander through the rest of the apartment.

"Where're you going?" Lily asked. She stopped as he opened a closet door inside one of the bedrooms. It wasn't very large, but the floor inside the closet was covered with a thick vanilla carpeting.

"Ahhh . . . ," Nate said and settled down inside the closet. "Now this is more like it." He reached inside his jacket and pulled out a comic book. Without a word, he began leafing through it. Lily leaned over. Inside were pictures and words typed so small she could barely make them out.

"What's that?" she asked.

"Doomsday Wars series," Nate said, flipping the page. "Book Two. It's the best one. Lex Luthor tries to get Brainiac to kill Superman, but it doesn't work."

"Brainiac?" Lily repeated.

Nate looked up in exasperation. "Yeah. Another enemy of Superman who wants to destroy him. He and Lex

Luthor get together and Lex Luthor gives the Brainiac extra powers in a lab experiment." Nate paused. "Now he's, like, unstoppable."

"Hmmm . . . ," Lily said. She stared at the pages over Nate's shoulder for a moment. "Where'd Superman come from anyway?"

Nate looked at her incredulously. "You mean from the beginning?"

Lily flushed. "Well, yeah. I don't know anything about the story, really. Is he from another planet or something?"

"Are *you* from another planet?" Nate asked. He rolled his eyes. "Who doesn't know about Superman?"

Lily stood up. "Forget it. Sorry I even asked."

Nate continued to leaf through his book. "Krypton," he said.

"What?"

"He came from the planet Krypton. In outer space."

"Then how'd he get here?"

"Krypton blew up. Superman's father knew it was gonna blow, so he put Superman—who was just a baby—in a rocket and shot him to Earth. Then these farm people, the Kents, found the rocket ship in a cornfield and raised Superman as their own kid."

"Why didn't his dad go with him?" Lily asked.

"What?"

"Superman's dad. You said he knew the planet was gonna blow up. So why did he just send Superman to Earth? Why didn't he go with him?"

"Because the rocket ship only had enough room for the *baby,*" Nate said. He shook his head. "Geez, you ask dumb questions."

"Why is that dumb?"

"Because it is," Nate said. "Everyone knows that if Superman's dad could've gone with him, he would've. *Geez.*"

"Maybe he wouldn't've." Lily crossed her arms. "You don't know."

Nate narrowed his eyebrows. "I got every single Superman comic ever made." He opened his arms. "*All* of 'em. So that means I know more about Superman than you will ever know in your whole life."

Lily rolled her eyes. "Okay, fine."

Nate opened the comic book again, but Lily could tell that he wasn't really reading. She walked around the edge of the room by placing the heel of one sneaker against the toe of the other. "Are you ever coming back to the store?" he asked suddenly.

Lily stopped walking. "To work?"

"Yeah," Nate said.

"Do you want me to?"

"*I* don't care," Nate said, flipping another comic page. "Pop was wondering, though."

Lily thought about what Mrs. Hiller had said about Bernard thinking the world of her. In a strange sort of way, she kind of missed him too. Now that she and Nate had saved three of Beatrice's eggs, the horrible reality of what happened to the rest of them didn't feel quite so horrible.

"Maybe," she said, looking back down at her shoes. "I have to think about it some more."

Nate shrugged and looked back down at his comic. "*I* don't care," he repeated. "Pop's the one who's wondering."

20

LILY HADN'T REALIZED JUST HOW MUCH she missed being at Pet Palace until Nate brought it up. And when he said that Bernard missed her, she knew she was close to making a decision. But it was bittersweet, knowing that the rest of Beatrice's eggs were in the trash somewhere, and that they had never been given a chance.

Bernard was thrilled to see Lily, giving her a big bear hug when she walked into the store the next day with Mrs. Hiller. Even Duke stood up on his hind legs and shrieked. "Boy, am I glad to see you!" Bernard said. Lily smiled and looked down at the floor. She wondered how glad Bernard would be if he knew she was hiding three of Beatrice's eggs.

Or that Nate had stolen them and brought them to her.

Mrs. Hiller ruffled her hair. "I'll be back in a few hours, dear. And remember, no walking home without me."

"Don't worry," Lily said. "I'll be here."

Bernard put his arm around Lily's shoulders and led her into the Reptile Room. "Beatrice laid her eggs, you know. Thirty-eight of 'em." He scratched his chin. "At least I think it was thirty-eight. I thought I counted forty-one when she first laid them, but I must have been mistaken." He steered her toward Beatrice's cage. "Look at her!" Bernard said, stopping in front of the terrarium. Beatrice was inside, resting underneath the wide heat lamp. "She looks good, don'tcha think?"

"Yeah," Lily said. She was glad Beatrice's eyes were closed. She didn't want to make eye contact with her.

"Now," Bernard said. "I'm going to give you a job in here. Nate's in the back, stocking shelves, but I think it's probably best that you and he work separately. I don't want any kind of repeat of what happened last week."

"Oh, Nate didn't do anything last week," Lily said quickly.

"He *didn't*? With that big ol' mouth of his?"

Lily shook her head. "No. Not at all. Nate and I get along fine. Seriously. You don't have to worry."

Bernard pushed out his bottom lip. "I really could use an extra set of hands in the storeroom," he said. "As long as you're sure."

"I'm sure."

"All right, then," Bernard said, turning around. "Follow me."

Sweat dripped down the sides of Nate's face as Lily and Bernard walked into the storeroom. There were boxes all over the floor, and the sides of the room had shelves that reached almost to the ceiling. Nate's hat was pushed back off his forehead, exposing a small tuft of damp hair. "Hey, Pop," he grunted, throwing a sack of birdseed into the corner.

"*Careful* with that!" Bernard barked. "What'd I tell you last week? You're gonna break one of them and then I'm gonna have to throw it all out again!" Duke stood up and chattered in his high-pitched monkey voice, scurrying from one of Bernard's shoulders to the other. Nate's chest heaved up and down. He glared at Duke.

Bernard gave Lily specific instructions about where to put the items that were still in the boxes and then turned to go. "You watch how you move those bags, Nate," he said, his hand on the door. "Remember what I said."

"Don't worry, Pop!" Nate stood up straighter and

pulled his hat back down. "I got it all under control!"

Bernard made a *harumpf* sound under his breath and walked out.

The air in the storage room was significantly warmer than the rest of the store. As Lily filled the shelves with boxes of hamster pellets and bags of sawdust, she felt herself beginning to perspire. Nate's face, already beet red, was getting redder by the minute. Dark wet circles appeared underneath his arms, and his neck was shiny with sweat. Lily wondered why he didn't take off his hat.

"You finish the Doomsday Wars series?" Lily asked, lining up blue bottles of flea and tick repellent.

Nate raised his eyebrows. He seemed surprised that Lily had remembered the title. "'Course," he said. "I read four of 'em every day."

"Wow," Lily said. "I can't even get through the first chapter of one book."

"What book?" Nate grunted as he lifted another bag of birdseed.

"*Alice in Wonderland*. I have to do a book report on it for school. I started it, but it's so weird. Not at all like the movie."

Nate turned around. The bag of birdseed was still in his hands. "Mama used to read that to me," he said quietly.

He let another bag of birdseed fall with a thud. "It was one of my favorites."

"Really?"

"Yeah," Nate said, leaning over to pick up another bag. "It's real good. My favorite is the Cheshire cat. He rocks."

"I just . . ." Lily struggled to explain herself. "I've never really read a book like that before. It seems so . . . hard."

Nate gave her a funny look. "Hard?" he repeated. "Why?"

Lily shrugged. "There's just so many . . . words."

"That's 'cause it's a *book,* dork."

"I guess." Lily sat back on her heels. She tried to remember the last book she had read, aside from the ones about lizards. Nothing came to mind.

"Whyn't you read it aloud to me?" Nate threw another bag into the corner. "Maybe it'll be easier that way."

"You think?" Lily asked.

"Yup. Bring it here when you come over."

"But how would I get my work done?"

"I'll do your work for you." Nate looked over at Lily's progress and rolled his eyes. "You're too slow anyway."

21

THE NEXT DAY, LILY WENT TO THE bathroom after lunch. It was empty. She always went to the bathroom before gym so she didn't have to get permission from Mr. Finkelsteiner to go. He looked annoyed when anybody asked to use the toilet.

She combed her hair, put on some cherry lip balm, and went into one of the stalls. After a few moments, she heard a flurry of activity. She peeked under the door. Amanda's leather boots were less than six inches away from her. Beside her boots, Lily could see Margaret Haggerson's tennis shoes, and Violet Landup's dirty pink jellies.

"I'm telling you, that girl isn't gonna know what hit her."

Lily sat frozen on the toilet seat as she listened to Amanda talk. "I got Clive to pound that little nerd friend of hers. Now it's her turn." She paused. "And this time, *I'm* gonna do it."

Violet scuffed the floor with the toe of her pink jellie. "She de*serves* it after the way she talked to you. You didn't even *do* anything!"

"Exactly." Lily heard a single clap, as if Amanda had just caught a fly between her hands. "It's about time somebody put her in her place."

Lily stayed in the locker room long after everyone had dressed and run out into the gym. She was tying her shoes for the fourth time, trying to get the laces just right. Gina was waiting for her.

"We gotta go, Lily." Gina's forehead was creased with lines. "Mr. Finkelsteiner is gonna give us detention if we're not out there when he blows the whistle."

Lily gave her laces a final yank and then stood up. "I heard Amanda talking in the bathroom," she said.

Gina's eyes got big behind her glasses. "About what?"

"About getting me. Today. During the game."

"What'd she say?" Gina asked.

"I think she's gonna try to hurt me," Lily answered. She tried to swallow over a lump in her throat, but it was too big. "She said it was time somebody put me in my place."

"Don't worry." Gina walked over to Lily and took her

hand. "Just stay close to me. If I see her . . ." She stopped talking as Mr. Finkelsteiner's whistle blew, and then clenched Lily's hand. "Come on! We have to go!"

It was their turn to be in the center of the circle for the second semifinal round of the dodgeball game. Lily knew she needed to do whatever it took to keep out of Amanda's line of vision and so she did her best to hide behind Gina, grabbing the hem of her shirt for balance. Gina didn't say a word; she was too focused on Amanda's next move. There was no mistaking that every time Amanda fired, it was headed straight for Lily's head. Luckily, she kept missing. After each of her throws, Mr. Finkelsteiner blew his whistle and waved his hands. "Waist and *under*!" he yelled. "One more time, Peterson, and you're on the bench!" Amanda nodded and then sneered at him behind his back.

Lily winced as she watched Clive wind up the ball. He aimed for Lionel Davis and nailed him squarely on the knee.

Lionel threw up his hands. "I wasn't even ready!" he yelled. "I didn't hear the whistle!" Lionel always argued whenever he got out. He had a hard time with losing.

Mr. Finkelsteiner jerked his thumb backward. "You're out, Davis!" Lionel kicked his way to the outside of the circle, muttering under his breath.

Lily couldn't be sure of it, but it seemed as though Clive and Amanda had some sort of plan in place. They had both stopped aiming for her, methodically taking out Lindsey Price, Ellie Tucker, and Randy Beaver instead. Suddenly, Lily realized what had happened. She and Gina were the only ones left standing inside the circle. Lily looked around, horrified. She'd never lasted this long during a dodgeball game. Ever. The rest of the fifth graders surrounded the two of them, waiting eagerly for their turn to throw. Amanda was breathing hard, her hands on her knees, as Clive patted the ball lightly between his sweaty palms. Without realizing what she was doing, Lily clutched Gina's wrist.

"Don't look right at Clive," Gina whispered, pushing Lily behind her. "Just keep him in your peripheral vision."

"My *what*?"

"Out of the corner of your eye," Gina said. "Keep track of him."

Mr. Finkelsteiner blew his whistle. "Let's go, kids! We have about ten seconds left before showers!"

Clive pretended to throw, and then turned and shot the ball over to Amanda, who grabbed it and flung it directly at the two girls. Lily heard a whistling sound as the ball flew past her. Gina leapt out of the way at the last possible second and the ball hit the bleachers and bounced away. Amanda screamed with rage. Clive punched the air and shouted a curse word.

Mr. Finkelsteiner blew his whistle. "Foul language! You're out, Bergen!"

Clive cursed again, this time under his breath, and stomped over to the bench.

"Last shot!" Mr. Finkelsteiner yelled. "Come on, guys! All you gotta do is hit one of 'em! The one left will duke it out next week with Amanda in the championship round!" He clapped his hands. "Let's play!"

Lily tried to stay calm, but the ball in Amanda's hands was starting to look like a bullet. She knew Amanda would aim for her. She was the easier of the targets, like a sitting duck out in the middle of a vast lake. She wondered if anyone had ever died from being hit too hard by a dodgeball. Maybe she would be the first.

She tried to focus, staying on her tiptoes the way Gina did so that she could bolt as soon as the ball left Amanda's hands. Amanda stood motionless across the wide expanse of shellacked floor. Her eyes seemed to glow blue, and when she inhaled, her nostrils flared wide. Lily knew she was taking her time, trying to psych her out. It was working. Sweat popped out like pimples on Lily's forehead and she thought she might throw up. Still, she kept her eyes on the ball, resting inside Amanda's hands like a bomb about to explode.

"Get back!" Lionel Davis was yelling again from the

sidelines. "Get back! You're too close! She's gonna . . ."

Bam! Lily heard the ball before she saw it, a low whistle as it cut through the air. It smashed so hard into her left knee that the right knee buckled, giving way beneath her like a sandbag in water. She was airborne for an eighth of a second before her face smashed against the gym floor. Her vision turned white with pain.

"Lily!" Somewhere behind her, Gina was screaming her name.

Then black.

22

LILY REPLAYED AMANDA'S FINAL SHOT at least twenty times that afternoon as she lay stretched out next to the iguana eggs in Willowood, staring up at the ceiling. Mrs. Hiller had given her a hard time about leaving the apartment after she showed up from school with a black eye. But Lily had managed to convince her that everything was all right.

She had spent most of the afternoon in the nurse's office with a bag of ice on her face and although her eyelid was swollen shut and the skin around it had turned a pale purple color, the nurse had assured her it would look a lot better in the morning.

The lids from the egg containers were placed neatly in a row beside the shoe box, and her shoes were off.

The sunbeams outside threw tiny patches of polka dots on the walls and the floor as it caught the glass from the chandelier.

If only Lionel Davis hadn't yelled from the sideline and thrown off her concentration. It was all Amanda had needed. Just a fraction of a second and *bam*!! Lily shook her head, forcing back tears that were collecting in the corners of her eyes.

She reached into her pocket and pulled out the picture of her father that she had retrieved a few nights earlier from beneath her dresser. There was still a thin film of dust along the front of it, despite the fact that she had wiped off the dust bunnies. Now she turned it facedown and rubbed it along the leg of her pants. She held it above her good eye. Her father stared back at her with his wonderful smile and his chipped tooth.

She pressed the picture against her shirt and tried not to cry. But the tears came anyway with a will of their own, stinging her sore eye and making her gasp. She rolled over, laying her cheek against the smoothness of the picture.

She stayed that way, without moving, for a long time.

23

BERNARD WAS PLEASED WITH THE JOB Lily and Nate did in the storage room. "I'm glad to see you two can work together after all," he said the next day. They were walking toward the backyard again, where there were at least twenty more hamster and gerbil cages stacked up under the lilac bush. "Now let's see you tackle the rest of the rodent cages."

"There's *more*?" Lily asked, aghast.

Bernard laughed. "I only gave you half last time. This is the other half." He paused, looking at Lily. "You sure you're up for working today with that eye?"

Lily nodded. The nurse had been right. The swelling had gone down considerably. Now it looked like a walnut was shoved under the skin of her temple instead of a lemon.

"Come on, then," Nate said. "Let's get to work." He turned as soon as Bernard shut the door. "You bring the book?"

Lily nodded and pulled it out from under her shirt. Nate grinned. His teeth were brown in some parts and uneven. "Sit under the tree," he said. "And you gotta start from the very beginning, in case I forgot anything. And speak up so I can hear good."

"Geez." Lily grinned as she made her way over to the tree. "You're bossy, aren't you?" She cracked open the book and pressed her nose against the pages. It smelled the way library books always smelled, like copper pennies and a little bit of bubble gum. "'Alice's Adventures in Wonderland,'" she read. "'By Lewis Carroll.'"

"I don't care who *wrote* it," Nate said. "Just read the story."

Lily ignored him. "'Chapter One.'" She flipped back to the table of contents. "Holy cow. Did you know there's *twelve* chapters?"

"Read," Nate ordered.

"All right, all right." Lily settled in, resting her back against the bark of the lilac bush, and began.

It was almost dusk when they heard Mrs. Hiller in the store, talking to Bernard. The sky overhead was gray with pink streaks along the bottom. Lily closed the book. Already, Alice had been down the rabbit hole, become tiny and then large again, and swam in the pool of tears. They were right in the middle of chapter three, which involved a Dodo bird and something called the Lory. Nate was right about reading it aloud. Lily had never read a book aloud. It seemed to create a lull of sorts as she went along. She felt sleepy and warm at the same time.

"I like it," she said.

Nate threw the last of the cages over into a pile. "Told you. And we haven't even gotten to the Cheshire cat yet. He's the best. He's so *sneaky*."

"I can tell I'm already gonna like Alice the best," Lily said. "She's so brave."

"That's just 'cause she's a girl," Nate said. "Girls always like the girls."

Lily shrugged. "Maybe." She grew thoughtful, thinking for a moment. "Nate?"

"Yeah?"

"What do you miss the most about your mom?"

Nate's face darkened. "You're not allowed to talk about Mama." His voice sounded forced, as if he were choking on the words. "Ever."

"Okay," Lily said. "I'm sorry. I didn't mean—"

"*Here* you are!" Mrs. Hiller swung open the door,

grinning broadly. She had a green scarf tied around her head and knotted under her chin. "You two have a good time?"

"Yeah." Nate stalked toward the door and pushed past Mrs. Hiller. "See you later."

Mrs. Hiller looked back at Nate and then turned around to face Lily again. "Everything . . . all right?" she asked.

Lily nodded. "Come on. Let's go home."

24

"HEY." GINA TURNED AROUND AND looked at Lily as Lily slid into her seat. "How's your eye?"

Lily winced, hoping no one else had heard Gina. "It's okay," she said. "It looks worse than it feels."

Gina stayed where she was, blinking a few times.

"What?" Lily asked. Gina tilted her head to one side and adjusted her glasses. "You got new glasses!" Lily said.

Gina grinned. "Do you like them?"

"They're red!" Lily answered, staring at the cherry-hued frames. They were much smaller than Gina's old brown ones. Lily could see her eyes clearly for the first time. They were small and black. She looked pretty. "I love them, Gina. They're awesome!"

"My dad says they make me look older," Gina said modestly. "Like I'm more mature."

Mrs. Bing rapped on her desk with a ruler.

"No more talking, class! We have two questions on the board that I want to discuss today. Who would like to read them aloud for me?" Amanda raised her hand, waving it in front of Mrs. Bing like a flag.

"All right, Amanda," Mrs. Bing said. "Go ahead."

Amanda cleared her throat. "'What's the most distinctive thing about you? And if you could change it, would you?'"

Jonathan raised his hand.

"Yes, Jonathan?" Mrs. Bing asked.

"What does 'distinctive' mean?" he asked.

"That's a very good question," Mrs. Bing answered. She surveyed the room. "Can anyone tell Jonathan what that word means?"

Gina raised her hand. "It means unique, or special," she answered.

"Excellent, Gina." Mrs. Bing's eyes began to flutter. "Would anyone like to share with the class a unique or distinctive thing about themselves?"

Jonathan raised his hand again.

"Yes, Jonathan?"

"I can fart really loud," he said.

"You're a slob," Amanda said, glaring at Jonathan. "A complete and total pig."

"Shut up, Amanda. Snot nose."

"Ex*cuse* me!" Mrs. Bing said. "This is unacceptable language, and I will not tolerate it in my classroom. Amanda and Jonathan, I'd like to see you after class, please." Lily caught Amanda's eye as she turned back around in her seat. She gave Lily an evil smile.

"Everyone take out a pencil, please," Mrs. Bing said. "I'd like you to think about how you will answer these two questions. We're going to begin with some brainstorming."

Clive raised his hand.

"Yes, Clive?" Mrs. Bing said wearily.

"I don't have a pencil," Clive said.

"What happened to the package of pencils I gave you on the first day of school?"

Clive shrugged. "I lost them all."

Mrs. Bing sighed heavily and then looked over at Gina. "Gina, do you have a pencil Clive could use, please?" Gina lifted the top of her desk and selected one of her neatly lined-up sharpened pencils for Clive. It was a glittery blue one with a green eraser.

Clive looked at it in disgust. "I'm not using this!" he said, throwing it to the floor. "This is a girly pencil!"

"Clive," Mrs. Bing said. "You are starting to get on my

last nerve. Does that concern you even a little bit?"

"No," Clive said. "I just need a pencil." Mrs. Bing clenched her jaw, snatched a pencil off her own desk, and thrust it at Clive.

"Take this," she said. "And I don't want to hear another word out of you." Clive slumped down in his seat. Mrs. Bing regarded the rest of the class. "Let's start by listing some things about ourselves that are unique," she said. "Who would like to start?" Clive raised his hand. "Forget it, Clive," Mrs. Bing said.

Amanda raised her hand. "Our house cost four hundred and twenty-five thousand dollars," she said.

Mrs. Bing sighed. "Is your house about you, Amanda?"

"Well, yeah," Amanda said. "I mean, I *live* there."

"But I'm asking you to think about something that has to do with you as a person. Not where you live, and not how much money your parents spent on your house."

Amanda scowled.

Gina raised her hand next.

"Yes, Gina?" Mrs. Bing asked.

"I have a scar on my arm that looks like a horse head," she said. "From when it got caught in the bread slicer at my dad's bakery."

"Let me see!" Jonathan said, getting up from his seat.

"Jonathan, sit *down*!" Mrs. Bing barked. Jonathan sat. Lily made a mental note to ask Gina to show her the horse scar at lunch. And to ask her a little more about her dad's bakery.

"That's a terrific example, Gina," Mrs. Bing said. "I'm sure no one else has anything quite like that on their arm." She turned and wrote the phrase "horse-shaped scar" on the board. "Who else?"

Jonathan raised his hand.

"I can burp the alphabet," he said. And before Mrs. Bing could stop him, he had opened his mouth and burped a loud, deep "Aaaaa." The class fell apart laughing.

"That's nothing," Clive said, leaping out of his seat. He threw his head back and belched the word "encyclopedia." It was so loud that it reverberated in Lily's ears.

"You're both complete pigs!" Amanda hollered.

"Clive, Amanda, and Jonathan will all stay after school for the rest of the week," Mrs. Bing said when things had quieted down again. "And if there is a further interruption from any of you, I will call Principal Winters down here immediately."

Mrs. Bing asked Margaret Haggerson to hand out clean sheets of paper.

"This will only be a first draft," Mrs. Bing said. "I

want you to write down anything that comes to mind about your own uniqueness. Don't worry about spelling or punctuation right now. You're not going to read this aloud. Just get something down. You have fifteen minutes."

Lily watched as Gina tucked her chin into her chest and began to write almost immediately. Her hair was separated down the middle into two neat ponytails. Lily could see the white of her scalp. She chewed on the end of her pencil and thought for a few minutes.

And then she began to write.

The most distinctive thing about me is my family. Or maybe I should say my half family, since I've never even once met my dad. The only reason I know what he looks like is because I have a picture of him that my mom doesn't know about. I keep it under my pillow at night. I've asked my mom a few times about him, but she doesn't give me any real answers. She says things like "I don't know" and "I guess so." I don't understand why he's not around when he knows that I was born. I mean, wouldn't you at least want to see someone who was part of you? I would.

Lily stopped writing, even though there were still five minutes left. She was tired. Her hand hurt from holding her pencil so hard. It was the first time she had ever written anything about her dad on paper.

She put her pencil down.

She didn't want to write anymore.

"So lemme see that horse scar of yours," Lily said to Gina at lunch. They were waiting in line to buy milk, since Mom had forgotten to pack Lily a drink. Gina pulled up the sleeve of her shirt and turned her arm over. The scar was much smaller than Lily thought it would be, but it definitely looked like the head of a horse.

Gina pointed to the top of it. "See, it has ears and everything."

Lily nodded, impressed. "And what happened again? Your arm got stuck in a blender?"

Gina looked at Lily like she was in first grade. "No, it didn't get stuck in a *blender*. I was helping my dad cut bread at his bakery and my sleeve got caught in the slicer." She ran two fingers over it gently. "Daddy says that I got lucky. One more inch, and I could've lost my arm." She shuddered and pulled her sleeve back down.

Gina called her father Daddy. Lily wondered if she had called him that since she had first learned how to talk.

She tried to imagine what Gina's father looked like. Did he wear glasses like she did? Was his hair as dark as hers?

"Where's your dad's bakery?" Lily asked.

"Magnolia Avenue," Gina said. "Right downtown. We live upstairs."

Lily nodded. "What's it called?"

"Doughn't You Know It," Gina said. She raised her eyebrows. "Get it?"

Lily laughed. "Yeah. That's a good one."

They got their milk and sat back down.

Gina fiddled with the snaps on her lunch box. "Hey, Lily?" She took out a container of chopped chicken and snow peas. The dishwater sauce was in the bottom again.

"Yeah?"

"Maybe you could come over some time after school. To my house, I mean."

"Oh, I don't know," Lily said. "I have a job."

"You do?" Gina sounded surprised.

"Yeah, I work at a pet store downtown."

"Pet Palace?" Gina asked.

"Yeah," Lily said, surprised that she knew it by name. "Have you ever been there?"

"Just once," Gina said. "My mom took me when she bought my little brother a goldfish. It died three days later."

"You probably didn't have the water at the right temperature."

"Probably," Gina said. She started to pick at her lunch box again. "So does that mean you're never free?" Lily felt uncomfortable. She definitely liked Gina, but she wasn't sure she wanted to start hanging out with her outside of school. They didn't really have that much in common. But she didn't want to hurt Gina's feelings.

"Maybe eventually," Lily said. "I mean, I kind of just started at Pet Palace. Maybe when I've been there awhile . . ."

Gina nodded her head. "I totally understand," she said. "Maybe when things slow down a little for you, then?"

Lily took a bite of peanut butter sandwich. It was soggy. "Yeah," she said. "Okay."

25

IT WAS FRIDAY. NATE AND LILY WERE IN the Kitty Korner part of the store, where Bernard had sent them to clean out the cats' cages. Luckily, this did not involve washing them; all that was required was a quick rubdown with a damp cloth. Nate was actually doing the cleaning while Lily sat atop one of the enormous bags of cat food, reading aloud from *Alice in Wonderland*. She had just finished chapter five, called "Advice from a Caterpillar."

Lily did not want to say so, but she thought the story was incredibly odd, even if it was all just from some guy's head. The way the people talked was weird and it was hard to understand.

"Now read slow," Nate ordered. He was inside the

largest of the kitten cages, squatting on his heels. "Chapter six is where Alice meets the Cheshire cat and I don't want to miss a *thing*."

"All right," Lily said. She read more slowly, hesitating here and there over a word she didn't recognize. Nate sighed in exasperation when this happened, but she ignored him. His mother had probably never stumbled over a word when she read, Lily thought, but she couldn't help it. She was only eleven, after all. And reading was hardly her best subject.

"Okay," Nate said after a while. "This is the best part. Read it *really* good."

It was a conversation between Alice and the Cheshire cat. Lily took a deep breath, trying to make her voice sound lively:

> *"What sort of people live about here?"*
>
> *"In* that *direction," the Cat said, waving its right paw round, "lives a Hatter, and in* that *direction," waving the other paw, "lives a March Hare. Visit either you like: they're both mad."*
>
> *"But I don't want to go among mad people," Alice remarked.*

"Oh, you can't help that," said the Cat, "we're all mad here. I'm mad. You're mad."

"How do you know I'm mad?" said Alice.

"You must be," said the Cat, "or you wouldn't have come here."

At this, Nate threw his head back and laughed. He laughed and laughed, holding his belly with both hands.

Lily closed the book. "What's so funny about all these people being mad at each other?"

Nate stopped laughing. "They're not mad *at* each other!" he exclaimed. "They're mad-crazy! Crazy-mad! The Cat says we're all crazy. That's what makes it so funny! He's smarter than everybody."

Lily frowned. She still didn't see the humor in it.

"I need you two to run over to the Super Fresh!" Bernard hollered from the other end of the store. "Duke is out of his favorite kind of lettuce and Clifford has a bunch of bones for the dogs!"

"Come on," Nate said, getting up and dusting himself off. "We can read the rest later."

"Who's Clifford?" Lily asked as they walked toward the

Super Fresh. It was the middle of October by now, a cool day with lots of sun. The trees were at the height of color, like small explosions of flame sitting atop smooth, brown legs.

"He's the butcher at Super Fresh," Nate said. "He saves all his bones for the dogs. And he gives me free salami."

"Oh." Lily kicked a pile of yellow and orange leaves and tried to stay out of Nate's way as he bounced along. He didn't seem to realize how unsteadily he walked.

"How're the eggs doing?" Nate asked.

Lily smiled. She felt all warm inside when she thought about them. "Good," she said. "I check on them every day, just like you said. They still look pretty much the same as when you brought them the first day."

Nate nodded. "That's good, then."

"Don't forget we have to get special lettuce for Duke," Lily said.

Nate scowled. "I hate Duke." Lily looked at him in surprise. The flaps of his red hat were snapped tightly under his chin. His cheeks puffed out on either side like a fish's.

"You hate him?" she repeated. "Why?"

"He's dumb."

"What do you mean? He's not dumb. He's a monkey."

"He's *dumb*!" Nate said loudly, looking straight ahead. "And stupid too!"

"You say everything is dumb and stupid," Lily said. "How come?"

"Because it is!"

"Okay," she said. "*Geez*, I was just asking."

She followed Nate as he walked straight back to the meat counter inside the Super Fresh. The farther they walked back into the store, the colder it got. Plastic-wrapped slabs of pink and red meat sat on piles of crushed ice, and a large wooden barrel was filled to the top with silver shrimp. A pudgy man with red cheeks and a white hat was behind the counter. He smiled as they walked up.

"Hey, Nate! Whatcha doin', guy?"

Nate beamed and stepped up to the glass. "Hi, Clifford! Pop said you got bones?"

Clifford held up an enormous package wrapped in white butcher paper. "You know I do!" He looked at Lily and jerked his head. "Who's this, Nate?"

"This is Lily," Nate said, taking the package of bones and arranging them under his arm. "She helps me and Pop at the store."

Clifford reached across the counter and stretched out his hand. "Nice to meetcha, Lily." Lily shook his hand. It was cold and clammy. Clifford grinned. He had a gold tooth in the front of his mouth. "You like salami too?" he asked. Lily nodded, just to be nice. She'd never tried it, but she thought it smelled an awful lot like toe jam.

Nate rose up on his toes in excitement. "I told you! Clifford always gives me salami."

Clifford laughed. He reached down and gave Nate another, much smaller, package wrapped in the same white paper. "Got it all ready for you, guy. It's the kind with the peppercorns in it, just the way you like it."

"Thanks, Clifford." Nate handed the package to Lily.

"You be sure to share, now," Clifford said, giving Lily a wink. "Don't eat it all, Nate."

"I won't!" Nate said, waving. "Bye!"

They grabbed two bags of romaine lettuce for Duke in the vegetable aisle and went up to the cashier to pay.

Nate reached into his pocket and pulled out the five-dollar bill Bernard had given him. "I'm rich." He fluttered the money at Lily.

"It's only five dollars," she said.

"Five dollars is *rich*," Nate said.

Lily looked at the cashier as she scanned Nate's bags of lettuce. She was very pretty with a short haircut and lots of silver rings on her fingers. Her name tag said CRYSTAL.

"Four twenty-nine," Crystal said, holding out her hand.

Nate hesitated and then looked at Lily.

"You have enough," Lily said. "Give her the five dollars."

"No." Nate clutched the paper bill. "She didn't say five dollars. She said four . . ."

Crystal blew a pink gum bubble and then popped it. "Four twenty-nine," she repeated.

"See?" Nate's voice was triumphant. "She didn't say five dollars."

"But you only have to pay four . . ." Lily looked at Crystal.

"Twenty. Nine." Crystal said impatiently.

Lily nudged Nate with her elbow. "Just give her the five-dollar bill. Trust me." Nate gingerly handed Crystal the bill, as if he was afraid of doing the wrong thing. Crystal took it, looking at Nate out of the corner of her eye. The cash register drawer opened with a ding and Crystal took out some change.

"Seventy-one cents is your change," she said, dropping the coins into Nate's palm.

"But I gave you dollars," Nate pleaded. "I have to get *dollars* back like last time."

"Oh, man," Crystal said.

Lily began to push Nate toward the automatic doors. People were looking as he started to raise his voice.

"Pop gave me dollars!" he said. "I need to get dollars back! He'll be mad!"

"Nate," Lily said, trying to keep her voice low. "Just relax, okay? I'll explain it to you when we get outside." But Nate kept yelling about his dollars. The automatic doors swung open.

And there, on the other side, was Amanda Peterson. She was with an older woman who had dark brown skin and black hair. She wasn't much taller than Amanda and she carried a large straw purse over her shoulder.

Amanda looked confused for a moment as she watched Nate, who was still walking ahead and yelling. Then she looked at Lily. The two girls locked eyes.

"Come on, Amanda," the woman said, grabbing a shopping cart. She spoke with a strange accent. "We're in a hurry."

"In a minute, Lucille," said Amanda, not dropping her eyes from Lily. "Go on ahead."

"Two meenits, Amanda!" Lucille said. "I want to see you in the fruit section in two meenits."

"All *right*!" Amanda replied fiercely. "I *heard* you!" She gave Lucille one of the looks she gave Lily in class. Lucille disappeared inside the store.

Amanda tilted her head to the side. "What are you doing still hanging around with that retard?"

It was definitely one of those times, Lily thought later,

that she should have ignored her. Mom always said that people who insulted others were just looking for attention. But Lily didn't ignore Amanda. And she didn't think about Mom or her advice until much later. All she could think about was whether or not Nate had heard Amanda use the word "retard."

She held her breath, watching him for a second. But he was still carrying on too loudly to hear much of anything. Lily wasn't sure if he even noticed Amanda standing there, looking at him as if he were some kind of cockroach.

And so she turned, balling her hands into fists. "Don't you ever use that word again. You don't even know Nate."

Amanda cocked her head. She had on an expensive leather jacket, a pink silk scarf tied around her throat, and a pair of shiny white ankle boots with pink fur around the top.

"What, and you do? Are you, like, actually *friends* with him or something?"

"Yeah," Lily said. "I am."

Amanda shuddered. "Oh, that is so gross." She curled her upper lip, looking at Nate. He was sitting on a wooden bench near the parking lot, his arms wrapped around the paper package of bones. "He's like, so . . . disgusting!"

"*You*'re so disgusting," Lily said. "Every time I look at you, I want to throw up." For a minute, she thought Amanda was going to take a swing at her, but she kept her hands by her sides. Then she licked her lips and smiled. But it wasn't a nice smile. It was one of those "just you wait" smiles.

"Well, you have fun with your little *friend*, then," she said. "I'll see you tomorrow in school." The automatic door swallowed her up before Lily could say another word. She gulped and looked down at her hands.

They were shaking.

26

THE NOTE STARTED DURING THIRD-period Social Studies. Amanda wrote it, and then sent it around. Anyone who was brave enough opened it, refolded it, and sent it along its way. They all did the exact same thing: first they looked at Lily, and then they began to laugh.

Finally the note made its way over to Gina. Jonathan, who knew that Gina would never open a note during class, threw it unfolded onto her desk as soon as Mrs. Bing turned around to write on the board. Gina jumped and stared at the note like it was a spider. Lily looked over her shoulder. It said: *Lily Sinclair loves a retard.*

Lily sat back and swallowed. She could feel Amanda's eyes from across the room, but she wasn't going to give her the satisfaction of looking up. Gina crushed the note into a ball and put it on the edge of her desk. Amanda slit her eyes at her.

"What is that on your desk, Gina?" Mrs. Bing asked, blinking furiously. She had a piece of yellow chalk in her hand.

"Um, nothing, really. Just something I have to throw out." Gina stood up and headed toward the garbage can. But Mrs. Bing held out her hand.

"Give it to me, please," she said. Lily felt her ears and cheeks start to burn. Now Mrs. Bing would read it. Would she laugh too? Gina sat back down as Mrs. Bing began to unfold the crumpled note. She read it quickly and then looked up at the class.

"Who wrote this?" she asked. No one said a word. Mrs. Bing crossed her arms. "I am going to give you three minutes to tell me who wrote that note," she said, her voice rising. "If no one comes forward, there is going to be big trouble." Lily glanced at Clive and Jonathan. They hated Amanda, but she knew they wouldn't rat on her. No one would. There wasn't a single person in the class who would be dumb enough to do that to Amanda Peterson.

"Amanda Peterson wrote it," Gina said suddenly. Lily's mouth dropped open. There was a little gasp from Amanda's side of the room. Her friends looked at her with wide eyes.

Amanda jumped out of her desk. "So what!" she yelled. "She does love a retard! I saw her with Nate Stump at the Super Fresh yesterday, and they were holding hands!"

Clive guffawed. "Nate Stump?" he repeated. "Man, that's disgusting!"

"Sit down, Amanda!" Mrs. Bing barked. Amanda sat, her lower lip quivering with rage. "And I don't want to hear another word from any of you. I'm disappointed and disgusted with your behavior." Mrs. Bing's blinking had finally stopped. She held up the note. "You have detention this afternoon, young lady. And if I ever see another note like this again, written about anyone, I will have you stay for two weeks' detention." She glared at Amanda. "Is that clear?" Amanda did not move. "Is that *clear*, Miss Peterson?"

"Yeah," Amanda muttered. "It's clear."

"And Lily," Mrs. Bing said, picking up her chalk again, "I'd like to see you after class."

After what seemed like forever, the fifth-period bell rang. Lily sat in her seat and jiggled her foot nervously as she waited for everyone to file out of the classroom for lunch. She wanted to get down to the cafeteria as soon as possible, in case Amanda started in on Gina. There was no telling what sort of retaliation she was going to take, now that

Gina had told on her. Finally, Mrs. Bing and Lily were alone.

"Come up here, Lily," she said, patting a chair next to her desk. "Have a seat." Lily sat down and began to work the inside of her cheek with her teeth.

Mrs. Bing leaned forward. Lily had never seen her this close-up before. She had pale purple circles under her eyes and she smelled like cinnamon breath mints and old coffee.

"Is Amanda Peterson giving you trouble?" she asked.

Lily looked at the floor and shook her head. "Not too much. I just try to ignore her."

Mrs. Bing folded her hands. "Well, I want you to let me know if she bothers you again."

"Okay," Lily said, although she knew she wouldn't.

Mrs. Bing cleared her throat. "Was Amanda telling the truth, Lily, when she said that she saw you at the Super Fresh with Nate Stump?" Lily nodded. "Are you friends with him?" Mrs. Bing pressed.

Lily nodded again. "I work at Pet Palace," she said.

Mrs. Bing bobbed her head up and down, as if she had suddenly made the connection. "And your mother knows this, of course?"

"Well, sure," Lily said. "Bernard . . . I mean, Mr. Stump wouldn't let me work there until I asked my mom's permission first." Mrs. Bing just kept staring at her.

Lily began to squirm. "So . . . um . . . do you know Nate?"

"Well, yes," Mrs. Bing said. Her blinking started again. "Sort of. I mean, everyone in Riverside Heights knows Nate." She paused. "Or at least they've heard of him."

"What do you mean?" Lily asked. "Is he famous or something?"

Mrs. Bing smiled. Lily wanted to reach out and rub the lipstick off her teeth, but she stayed still. "I guess you could say that. A few years back his mother died and Nate went . . ." Mrs. Bing stopped and put her finger to her lips. "How should I put this delicately? He went a little bit off the deep end, I guess you could say."

Lily thought about what Mrs. Hiller had told her about Bernard having to put Nate into a home for a little while. "Yeah," she said. "I think I heard something about that."

Mrs. Bing reached out and put her hand over Lily's. "Lily, I want you to promise me that you'll be careful." Lily looked at her teacher. She wasn't blinking anymore, but the serious look on her face was scaring her.

"Why?"

"Because Nate got pretty violent that time. He had to be taken away by the police and put in a special home after he destroyed his father's apartment."

"Destroyed his father's apartment?" Lily repeated. She couldn't imagine Nate destroying anything, let alone a whole apartment. But Mrs. Bing was nodding. "One night he just smashed everything to bits with a metal pipe," she said. "It was in the news and everything." Lily stared at her hands. "Of course, that was five years ago," Mrs. Bing said. "But I don't know if that kind of violent behavior ever really leaves someone." She lifted Lily's chin with two fingers so that she was looking at her. "So just be careful, all right, Lily? Promise me?"

"Okay," she said. "I will. Can I go now?"

"You certainly may," Mrs. Bing said.

Lily turned and fled the room.

Principal Winters was in the cafeteria when Lily finally got there. He was talking to Amanda next to the soda machine.

"It was an accident!" Amanda kept saying. Her wide blue eyes were welling up with fake tears. "I didn't mean to do it! I swear! I didn't even see them!" Four of her friends stood a little ways off, nodding their heads like dolphins as Amanda spoke.

"Accident or no accident," Principal Winters said, "your parents are going to be called so that I can inform them of your behavior. I'm going also going to request that they replace Gina's glasses." He looked sternly at Amanda. "This is the third time this year that I've had to leave my office and come down here because of you, young lady. Enough is enough."

Principal Winters was really chubby. He got out of breath when he walked down the hall and he wore ties that were way too short for his shirts. His squishy brown shoes made a squeaking sound when he walked. Still, whenever Lily passed him in the hall, he always waved and smiled at her. She thought he was one of the nicest principals she had ever met. Now she liked him even more.

Lily scanned the room for Gina, but she was nowhere to be found. She ran into the bathroom. It looked empty.

"Gina!" she yelled. "Are you in here?" Her voice echoed against the blue tile. She heard a sniffling sound from the very last stall.

"Gina?" she asked again, softly this time. "Is that you? Are you okay?" The door swung open as Gina kicked it from inside. She was sitting on the floor next to the toilet, her knees drawn up to her chest. Her new glasses were in her hands.

Lily squatted down next to her on the cold floor. "What happened? What did she do to you?"

Gina rubbed her eyes. She started to say something, but her voice broke and she began to cry again. "It was so embarrassing, Lily!"

Lily rubbed her shoulder. "Did she hurt you?"

"She flipped my skirt up," Gina said. Her voice was different now, angry. "I was coming back from the milk line and she grabbed it and pulled it up so that everyone could see my underwear."

Lily felt a heat start to rise from the bottom of her belly.

"In front of everyone!" Gina sobbed. She held up her glasses. They were split in two and one of the lenses had popped out. Gina held it in her hand like a broken eggshell. "I turned around so fast that I dropped my lunch and then my glasses fell off and when I reached out to get them, she stepped on them! On *purpose*!"

The inside of Lily's mouth tasted bitter.

"My dad worked a long time to save up for these glasses," Gina said. "I had to wear those old brown ones forever until he got enough money to get these. I don't how I'm going to tell him . . ." Her voice drifted off.

There was no way Amanda was going to get away with this, Lily thought to herself. Gina had taken a huge risk standing up for her in class the way she had—and she had paid the price. They had to do something. It was them against Amanda now.

"Listen to me," Lily said, rubbing Gina's back. "I'll figure something out. I promise. Everything will be all right."

27

BERNARD WAS AT THE CASH REGISTER when Lily came in after school. He was shaking his head and scratching his stomach at the same time.

"Hi!" Lily said. "Is everything okay?" Duke scurried up next to Bernard's ear and began to nibble on it.

Bernard growled and swatted him away gently. "No, everything is not okay. Nate and I just got into our twenty-seventh argument of the day and he stormed upstairs. Maybe you could go and talk to him."

"Me?" Lily asked.

"Well, sure," Bernard said gruffly. "You're the only person he talks about, besides his cats. Give it a shot, eh?"

Duke began to make his little high-pitched squealing sounds.

"Oh, shut up, you old thing," said Bernard, swatting at him.

Nate talks about me? Lily thought as she climbed the enormous staircase up to the apartment where Nate and Benard lived. *Why? And what kinds of things does he say?*

She began to count the steps as she got closer to the apartment. Twenty-nine in all. By the time she reached the top, she was panting hard. Lily knocked on the door. No answer. She knocked again, harder this time. She could hear Nate walking around inside. His footsteps got closer and closer and then they stopped just outside the door.

"Nate?" she called.

"Who is it?"

"It's Lily! Can I come in?"

"How do I know it's Lily?" Nate asked.

"What do you mean?" Lily was confused. "You know my voice, Nate! It's me!"

"Mama said never open the door to strangers."

"Nate, come on. I'm not a stranger. I've been working in the store with you for almost a month now!"

"I can't see you," Nate said. "I can't tell."

Lily thought hard. Then she leaned in close to the door. "I know who your favorite character in *Alice in Wonderland* is," she whispered.

There was no answer.

"It's the Cheshire cat," Lily said, a little louder this time. "Because he can disappear and not even Superman can do that."

The door opened a crack.

Nate peeked out.

Lily waved. "Hey," she said softly. "Can I come in?"

Nate opened the door a little wider. He had his red hat turned around backward for some reason. It sat on his head like a big watermelon. A small black cat with white markings around his mouth was curled up in his arms. Lily reached out to pet him, but Nate turned around.

"Don't touch Julius," he said. "He's not feeling well."

"What's the matter?" Lily asked. "Are you mad at me?"

"Nope."

"Then who are you mad at?"

"Pop," Nate said, stroking the cat with his hand. Julius purred loudly under his touch.

"Why?" Lily asked. "What happened?"

"He's mean," Nate said. "He's mean and I hate his guts." Lily didn't know what to say to that. She knew it wasn't nice, but she certainly knew what it was like to hate someone's guts. Amanda had made sure of that. But she felt bad hearing Nate say such a thing about his father.

"Why?" she asked.

"I don't wanna talk about it," Nate said.

"Okay." She tried to change the subject. "I've never seen your apartment before. Can you show me around?"

"Okay," Nate said glumly. He led Lily into the front room, which had a low ceiling and blue walls. A tiny TV and a VCR were pushed up against the opposite wall, and the couch was a plushy brown. A glass coffee table, which was in front of the couch, held a leaf-shaped ashtray.

Lily wrinkled her nose. "Ugh, does your dad smoke?"

"Cigars," Nate said. "They stink."

"They sure do," Lily said.

"Mama never let Pop smoke. She said it wasn't good for my lungs." Nate's face was scrunched up into a scowl. "But he doesn't care now."

"My mom smokes," Lily said. "She's been trying to quit ever since I was little, but she always starts again. She's always sneaking them and she thinks I don't know." She stared out the window. "I don't know why adults think we're stupid."

"Your mom thinks you're stupid?" Nate asked.

Lily shrugged. "She never tells me the truth about stuff."

"What stuff?"

"Like when she smokes." Lily paused. "And why my dad left after I was born."

"It's bad to lie," Nate said somberly. "Lex Luthor lies

all the time so that he can trap Superman." He paused. "I *always* tell the truth."

Julius lifted his head suddenly and then jumped out of Nate's arms.

"Hey!" Nate yelled. "Get back here, Julius! It's quiet time for you!" He ran after the cat, down a narrow hallway into another room. Lily followed. Julius had jumped up onto a pillow on top of a large bed. He was pressing the pillow lightly with his paws, as if he were kneading a pile of bread dough.

Nate sat down next to him and stroked the top of his head. "Julius always knows when it's quiet time," he said, looking at me. "That's why he gets on my bed."

Lily nodded and looked around. "Is this your room?"

"Yeah," Nate answered. The room was big. Nate even had his own bathroom off to one side. The entire wall above his bed was covered with *Superman* posters. There were big ones of him flying with one clenched fist in the air, small ones of him standing over different enemies, and a medium-size one of him lifting a car above his head. Muscles bulged under his blue and red suit like thick ropes.

The other walls were covered with pictures of cats. Some were sitting in the middle of large green fields; others had big floppy hats on top of their heads. A few of them even looked like they were smiling. Above Nate's headboard was a poster of an orange and white tabby cat dangling in midair, its paw attached somehow to the string of a floating blue balloon. Underneath its legs, in big black letters, it said HANG ON!

Nate got up off the bed and walked over to his dresser. Dipping his hand into a glass jar full of paper clips, he grabbed a fistful and began to drop them slowly back into the jar. Then he did it again. And again.

Lily walked over to stand next to him. That's when she saw the picture. It was lying next to the paper clip jar, loose and unframed. The woman smiling out from it had curly dark hair and big eyes. Little round earrings shone against her earlobes. Her face was shaped exactly like Nate's, and her lips turned up at the corners, the way Nate's did. Only her eyes, which were not narrow like Nate's, were different.

"Is that your mom?" Lily asked, picking up the picture.

"Hey!" Nate snatched it out of her hands. "Don't touch that!" Julius picked his head up off the pillow and pricked his ears.

Lily stepped back. "Geez, Nate. You don't have to bite my head off. I didn't know."

Nate arranged the picture behind the paper clip jar so that it was standing up. "Don't ever touch Mama," he muttered. "You're not allowed."

Lily turned to go. It was stupid of her to come up here, she thought, and even stupider of Bernard to think that she could do anything to make Nate feel better. Nate didn't think the world of her. He probably thought she was just as annoying as his dad.

"I'll see you later," she said, staring at Nate's back as she walked out of the room. She wanted him to turn around. To apologize. To say anything. But he didn't. Julius licked his paws and settled back down into Nate's pillow.

Stupid old cat, Lily thought. *Weemis is cooler than you any day.* She opened the door and headed back down the stairs.

"Lily?" Nate was standing in the doorway, twisting his hands around each other.

"Yeah?"

"Did you bring the book?"

Lily smiled a little. She patted her stomach where the book was jammed in the waistband of her pants. "Yeah."

"Will you . . . ?" Nate hesitated. "Read some more?"

Lily paused. What had Mrs. Hiller said? That Nate's brain was like an eight- or nine-year-old's? She needed to be more patient, maybe give him more of a break.

"All right." Lily went back to Nate's room and sat down with her back against his bed. He sprawled out on the floor across from her, turning his red hat around and then pulling it down over his eyes.

"'Chapter seven,'" she began. "'A Mad Tea Party.'"

28

MAYBE AMANDA WAS GETTING TIRED OF them, Lily thought. Or maybe she was scared of getting expelled from school. Lily knew Amanda's parents had come in, as well as Gina's parents, after Mr. Winters had called them both in to discuss the situation. Perhaps that had had some kind of impact. Either way, a whole week had gone by and Amanda hadn't bothered Gina or Lily at all.

Then, at lunch on Tuesday, as Lily leaned over the metal railing, trying to get her fingers around a container of milk, Amanda reached over, grabbed the carton, and handed it to her. Lily stood there, speechless, but Amanda had already turned back around.

"What do you think it is?" Lily asked Gina as she peeled open her sandwich bag. Gina's plastic container was filled with slices of grilled chicken, tomato, lettuce, and slivered almonds. She also had her usual bottle of water and a chocolate fudge cookie. Lily took a bite of her peanut butter sandwich and a sip of milk. "Do you think Amanda's just scared of getting expelled?"

"Who cares?" Gina's mouth was full of chicken. "As long as she isn't bothering me, I'm not going to worry about it." Lily stared at Gina's glasses. She'd been surprised when Gina told her that her parents had refused Amanda's father's offer to replace her glasses. They weren't trying to be rude, Gina explained, but accepting that kind of monetary help would be an insult to their family. Her father had managed to pop the lens back in and had taped the frame together with red tape so that it was hard to tell that they were broken unless you looked closely. Still, it puzzled Lily that the Soo family wouldn't accept a brand-new pair of glasses for Gina—even if they were going to be paid for by the parents of the biggest snob at school.

"Why do you think she's so mean?" Lily asked. "The only thing I ever did was giggle a little about her middle name."

"People who are sad are always mean," Gina said.

"She's not *sad*." Lily looked at Gina like she was crazy. "In case you haven't noticed, she's got everything! Clothes, looks, money, awesome hair. *And* she's popular."

But Gina was shaking her head. "She doesn't have everything. She never sees her parents."

"What are you talking about?" Lily asked. "She's always going on and on about how her parents take her on all these amazing trips overseas and—"

"That's once a year. I don't think she sees them at all the rest of the time." Gina chewed thoughtfully. "My dad told me they both work these really crazy jobs and are always flying around the country on business trips."

"So who takes care of Amanda?" Lily asked.

"They have a housekeeper who lives there," Gina said. "She comes into the bakery all the time to buy bread. She's friends with my dad and she tells him all this stuff. I think he said she's from Mexico or something."

Lily thought back to the day at the Super Fresh when she had seen Amanda with the dark-skinned woman. What had Amanda called her? Lucille?

She took another bite of sandwich and chewed hard. It still wasn't a good enough excuse, she decided. At least Amanda *had* both of her parents. Even if they weren't around all that much. Lily hardly saw her mother at all, except on weekends, and at this point, she wasn't even sure if her father was still alive.

That was a lot worse than what Amanda had to deal with.

Wasn't it?

29

LILY BEGAN TO JUMP UP AND DOWN when she saw Aunt Wava's curls, which, even smushed down under a big brown cowboy hat, still stuck out on all sides like an overgrown pricker bush. "Here!" she yelled, running toward her in the bus station. "We're over here!"

Aunt Wava dropped her bag and held out her arms, just like she always did whenever she saw Lily. She was wearing a little denim jacket, orange corduroy pants, and chunky black boots with buckles on the sides. Lily jumped into her arms and wrapped her legs all the way around her. She smelled like bubble gum and turpentine. "Oh!" Lily said. "I'm so glad you're finally here!"

"Me too," Aunt Wava said. "Mugga-mugga?" They rubbed noses, which was a little thing Aunt Wava had done with Lily ever since she was a baby.

Lily pulled her head back. "What's in your nose?"

"I got it pierced," Aunt Wava said. "Do you like it?" Lily leaned in and examined the silver hoop. It was so thin that she hadn't even noticed it until she got up close.

"It's cool!" she said. "Is it in there for good?"

Aunt Wava put Lily down slowly. "Well, I can take the ring out, but the hole's there for good." She stared at Lily for a moment. "My goodness, Lily, you're gigantic! Look at you!" She looked at Mom. "Claire! Why didn't you tell me Lily'd gotten so tall? And so gorgeous?" Aunt Wava always said Lily was gorgeous. Lily didn't believe her, since people who were related to you had to say those kinds of things. Still, it was nice to hear.

Lily grabbed Aunt Wava's hand. "Come on!" she said, pulling her toward the street. "I can't wait till you see our new place!"

Lily tried desperately to get Aunt Wava to herself after they got back to the apartment, but it wasn't an easy thing to do when Mom was involved. Since Aunt Wava was Mom's only sister, Mom always wanted to talk, or as she called it, "catch up," whenever Aunt Wava came to visit. Unfortunately, her idea of "catching up" could take hours, or sometimes even days.

"If it seems like I'm hogging Aunt Wava this weekend, it's just because I haven't seen her in six months," Mom had said the night before, when she tucked Lily into bed. "She needs to talk about all her anxieties about the show. Plus, we have a lot of catching up to do."

"I want to catch up with her too," Lily said.

Mom smiled and kissed her on the forehead. "I know, sweetie. We'll just have to share her."

Except that Mom wasn't sharing. They were in the kitchen, already on their second pot of coffee. Mom had just told Lily for about the fortieth time to go watch TV, since they needed to talk about some personal things.

"I'm gonna go downstairs," Lily said, giving up after a while.

"Okay," Mom said, not turning around.

"What's downstairs?" Aunt Wava asked, leaning to the side.

"Just the back porch," Lily said. "It's sort of my place."

Aunt Wava nodded and grinned. "We'll talk later, okay, pumpkin?"

I hope so, Lily thought, as she quietly let herself into Willowood. She had to ask Aunt Wava something really important. But she didn't want Mom to find out. Or anyone else for that matter.

She unscrewed the lids to the iguana containers and stared down at the smooth, leathery shells.

Twenty-nine more days.

Aunt Wava made reservations at a fancy Japanese place downtown for dinner. Mom got all dressed up in her red skirt and white scoop-neck blouse and her black high heels with the straps across the front. Lily put on a clean pair of jeans and a blue T-shirt. She slid her black sneakers under her bed and took out her blue sequined mary janes with the chunky little heels. They were one of her favorites. Aunt Wava wore the same orange corduroy pants, but she changed into a long-sleeved black shirt and a pair of gold wedge shoes with open toes. Her toenails were painted a pale violet. She yanked a brush through her curls and kept brushing until her hair shone like copper under the light.

"You look amazing, Aunt Wava!" They were walking toward the restaurant. It was a cold night, and everyone was moving fast. Mom's heels made a clicking sound on the sidewalk. Lily could smell Mom's perfume, rich and sweet, above her.

Aunt Wava squeezed Lily's hand. "Thank you, pumpkin. You look pretty fancy yourself. Those shoes are amazing."

That was one of about a million things that Lily loved about Aunt Wava. She always, no matter what, noticed her shoes.

Katana's was the fanciest place Lily had ever been to. They were seated at a table with a red velvet tablecloth. There were silk fans on the walls and a huge fountain that came right up out of the floor. The waiters wore beautiful jackets with pictures of trees and houses all over them and tiny black slippers on their feet. Lily kept giggling because they put their hands together and bowed whenever they came over to their table.

Aunt Wava and Mom ordered big blue drinks with orange slices on the sides and Lily got a Shirley Temple with a cherry. Then, since Mom and Lily didn't have any idea what anything on the menu was, Aunt Wava ordered for everybody.

Pretty soon, a waiter began placing tiny plates of sushi and other weird things called California rolls in front of them. The sushi looked like pink tongues, and the California rolls, which were black on the outside, were white and sticky in the middle. Mom and Lily looked at each other. They put a piece of each of their plates and stared at it nervously. Aunt Wava said she ate sushi just about every day in New York.

But it didn't sit well with Lily. She gagged when

she tried one of the smooth pink pieces and, after Aunt Wava told her it was raw fish, she pressed her napkin hard against her lips so that she wouldn't throw up. The California roll wasn't too bad. It tasted a little like cream cheese. Still, Lily shook her head when Aunt Wava offered her another one.

"Tell you what," Aunt Wava said, flipping open the menu again. "I bet they have some great miso soup here."

Lily wiped her lips. "Miso?"

"Yes." Aunt Wava tapped the menu with her finger. "Right here. I'm going to get you one of those, pumpkin. It's just broth and a few vegetables, which you don't even have to eat. You'll like it. I promise."

"This girl I know at school has miso soup sometimes for lunch." Lily took a sip of her Shirley Temple.

Mom arched an eyebrow. "She does?"

"That's fantastic!" Aunt Wava said. "Is it homemade or does it come out of a can?"

"Oh no," Lily answered. "Her mom makes it. She makes all her lunches. From scratch, I think."

"Like what?" Aunt Wava inserted a large piece of orange fish into her mouth with her chopsticks. "Tell me. I love to hear what people eat for lunch."

"Oh, everything. Noodles with peanuts and vegetables . . ."

"Yum!" Aunt Wava said. Her green eyes sparkled. "Sounds delicious. What else?"

"Salads with, like, orange slices and hard-boiled eggs . . ." Lily shuddered. "Chicken sometimes, with almonds, miso soup, rice with peas. . . . Oh, and every day, she brings a different cookie." Lily made a circle using the fingers on both hands. "And they're, like, *this* big. Her dad's a baker. He owns a shop downtown. He makes them."

"Wow!" Aunt Wava said. "Are you lucky to be friends with someone like *that*, or what?"

Just then, a waiter brought Lily's soup, placing the blue-and-white china bowl down in front of her with a flourish. There were little white squares of something Lily didn't recognize, as well as small green circles floating around in the broth. Lily wrinkled her nose. "What's in there?"

Aunt Wava leaned over. "Oh that's just some tofu and scallions. You don't have to eat them if you don't want. Just drink the broth. I'm telling you. It's yummy."

Lily stirred her soup as Aunt Wava began to tell Mom a funny story about the guy who owned the art gallery where she was having her show. Carefully avoiding the white squares and green circles, she spooned a tiny amount of the broth into her mouth and sipped it slowly. It was just warm enough, with a soft, salty taste to it. Mom and Aunt Wava were laughing hysterically.

Lily took another sip.

And then another.

Before she knew it, the bowl was empty.

30

LILY WOKE UP THE NEXT MORNING TO the sound of Aunt Wava and Mom talking in the kitchen. She pulled the covers over her head. Adults were always telling kids to be quiet, she thought, when *they* talked more than anyone. It was so unfair.

She got up and checked on Weemis. He was sitting on his rock, watching her. She lowered her hand in gently and let him crawl along her knuckles.

"Hey, little guy. How've you been? I haven't been paying much attention to you lately, have I?" Weemis blinked and cocked his head. Lily ran her fingernail over the glide of his tail. "I'm sorry, buddy. You know I love you." She lowered him back down and he slid off, scrambling his feet into the soft sand.

There was an extra-large decaf with cream and sugar and four chocolate-glazed Munchkins waiting for Lily on the kitchen table. Mom's and Aunt Wava's cups were nearly empty. A half-eaten bagel with cream cheese sat on a plate in the middle of the table. Mom pointed to the extra-large coffee. "For you, sweetie."

Lily grabbed it. "Thanks," she said, slurping the hot liquid.

"You're welcome." Mom stood up. "Now, I have to go do some grocery shopping. I'm making your favorite dish tonight, Wava, in honor of your gallery show."

"Enchiladas?" Aunt Wava asked.

Mom nodded and grinned. "I've gotta go get avocados, cilantro, and tortillas. I've got everything else I need here." She paused. "I think."

"Can we stay here?" Lily asked. "Just me and Aunt Wava?"

Mom nodded. "I thought you might want a little one-on-one," she said, pushing her purse up along her shoulder.

Finally.

"I have a favor to ask you," Lily said, after Mom left for the store.

Aunt Wava raised her eyebrows. She was wearing Mom's fuzzy green bathrobe. It made her eyes look even greener. Her hair hung in matted coils along her shoulders. "What is it, pumpkin?"

"Can you draw me a picture?"

"Of course," Aunt Wava said. "What kind of picture?"

"The portrait kind," Lily answered. "You know, like what you did for your show."

"Ohhh," Aunt Wava said. "And who do you want a portrait of?"

Lily pulled the picture of Nate's mother out of her pocket and put it on the table. "My friend Nate's mom. I want to surprise him."

"This is sort of blurry," Aunt Wava said, picking up the picture and studying it.

"I know," Lily said. "That's why I was thinking you could make him an even better one. Bigger, maybe, and really clear."

Aunt Wava was nodding. She held the picture out at arm's length and cocked her head to one side.

"And another thing," Lily said. "Could you do it today?"

Aunt Wava's mouth fell open. "To*day*? Oh, honey, I don't think . . ."

Lily bit her lip. "I kind of took that picture without Nate knowing and I don't want him to find out." She said the words in a rush, trying to get them out of her as fast as possible.

"You took it without asking?" Aunt Wava repeated. "Why?" Lily's face got red. She knew she couldn't explain everything to Aunt Wava right now. She probably wouldn't ever tell anyone how she had asked Nate to get her a glass of water that afternoon while she was reading chapter eight so he would leave the room, or how she had grabbed the picture of his mother, putting it in between the final chapters of *Alice in Wonderland* so that he wouldn't suspect.

"He would've gotten upset if I asked him," she said instead. "He's a little . . . different. He's got Down syndrome."

"Well, just because someone has Down syndrome doesn't mean he won't be upset about someone stealing his things," Aunt Wava said. She looked at Lily with a serious expression. Lily began to bite the inside of her cheek.

"I don't *want* it to be stealing," she said. "I'm going to put it back today, when I go to work. That's why I need you to do it so fast. Do you think you could do it that fast?"

Aunt Wava looked at Lily for a long time without saying anything. Then she handed her the picture.

"Let's go," she said. "My paints are in the other room."

31

IN TEN MINUTES, AUNT WAVA HAD changed into her old jeans and a T-shirt, set up her portable easel in the kitchen where she said the best light was, and sketched a picture of Nate's mother. Watching Aunt Wava work reminded Lily a little of watching a bird fly. She moved her hands the way birds moved their wings, as if they knew exactly how hard they needed to push, how many times they needed to flap, while at the same time knowing exactly where they were going. It was amazing.

The picture of Mrs. Stump was just in pencil, but Lily would have taken it right then and there, it was so good. Aunt Wava even darkened the little round earrings in her ears so that they stood out exactly the way they did in the picture. It was even better than the photograph.

"Wow!" Lily said, as Aunt Wava held up the picture and tilted her head to look at it. "It's incredible."

"No." Aunt Wava lay it down again on the kitchen table. "Something's not right with the eyes." She began to work again, crouching down in front of the easel, a thin pencil in her hand. "How about some music, pumpkin?" she asked. "I always have something on when I work."

Lily went over to the counter and turned on the radio. "Dancing Queen" by ABBA was playing. It was one of Mom's favorite songs.

"Oh, turn it up!" Aunt Wava said, putting down her pencil and twisting her hair into a knot at the back of her neck. "I love this song!" Lily turned up the radio. The song came blaring through the little space of the kitchen. Aunt Wava began to swing her hips from side to side. Then she put down her pencil and held out her hands. Lily grabbed on tight and sang along, although she wasn't sure of a lot of the words. Aunt Wava twirled her around the kitchen and laughed. They were both breathless when the song ended. Aunt Wava's face was beet red. Lily filled two glasses with water and handed one to her. Aunt Wava gulped down the water, asked for another, and plopped down into one of the kitchen chairs.

"Aunt Wava?" Lily asked as she refilled her glass.

"Yes?"

"Can I ask you something?"

Aunt Wava picked up a thin paintbrush and swirled it around a little blob of peach-colored paint. "Anything."

"Why don't adults tell the truth about some things?"

Aunt Wava stopped swirling her paintbrush and looked at Lily. "Are you talking about me?"

"No!" Lily said. "No way! I don't think you'd ever lie to me!" She handed Aunt Wava the glass of water. Aunt Wava tilted it back and drained the whole thing in one swallow.

"Your mother, then?" she said finally.

Lily looked away.

"Lily, what do you think your mother isn't being straight with you about?"

Lily stepped on her shoe.

"Pumpkin?"

"My dad, okay?" Lily said. "I've asked her a bunch of times to just tell me the truth about him and she won't. All she ever says is that she doesn't know! And I know she's lying, because she thinks I'm too young or that I can't handle it or that I'm just stupid or something!"

Aunt Wava wiped her lips slowly with the back of her wrist and then patted her lap.

"I don't want to," Lily said. "I'm not a baby anymore."

"Fine," Aunt Wava said. "Then if you're not a baby anymore, why can't you accept that maybe the answer your mother is giving you is the only one she's got?"

"Because it's not!" Lily yelled. "It can't be. There's a reason for everything. You can't just say 'I don't know where he is,' or 'I don't know what happened.' That's not fair!"

"Lily," Aunt Wava said. "There are lots of situations in the world that we have no answers for."

"Like what?" Lily mumbled.

"Like why was Nate born with Down syndrome and you weren't?"

Lily bit her lip.

Aunt Wava was right; there was no answer for that one. It was just the way it was. Aunt Wava reached out and pulled Lily onto her lap. This time, Lily didn't object.

"You know, Lily, when you were in first grade and asked your mom about your father, she called me. She was worried that she was handling it badly, and she wanted to know if I thought she should have made something up, or maybe even have told you that he had died."

"She did?"

Aunt Wava nodded. "She was embarrassed that she didn't know. She said that you deserved a better answer. She wanted to tell you something that you could kind of hold on to. Not knowing where someone went or why he went away is hard. But she wanted to be honest with you from the very beginning, even when you were too young to understand the answers."

"So the answer really is that she just doesn't know?" Lily asked.

Aunt Wava nodded. "That's the real answer," she said. "The honest-to-God truth. One day he was there, and the next day he wasn't. And she hasn't heard from him since."

"But I don't *want* that to be the answer," Lily said, as the tears came again. "It's not enough!"

"It's all she has," Aunt Wava said, kissing her on the ear. "It's all she can give you, honey." Lily rested her cheek along the smooth part of Aunt Wava's neck.

"That sucks," she said softly.

Aunt Wava smoothed her hair. "It does suck," she said. "It sucks big-time."

Lily settled against Wava's chest, listening to her heart beat underneath her soft shirt. She didn't know yet if she believed what Aunt Wava said, but hearing it made her feel a little better.

A loud banging on the door made them both jump.

"Lily! Are you in there?" It was Bernard's voice. He sounded panicked. Lily ran over to the door and flung it open. Bernard and Mrs. Hiller were standing in the hallway. Bernard opened his mouth, but nothing came out. Mrs. Hiller put her arm on his shoulder.

"Lily," she said. "Do you know where Nate is? Have you seen him today?"

"No," Lily replied. "I'm not supposed to go in today until four. Why? What's wrong?"

Bernard drew his hands down slowly along his cheeks and slumped to the floor.

"What's wrong?" Lily asked again as Aunt Wava came up behind her.

Bernard's eyes looked wild, like he was frightened and angry at the same time. "He . . . he just went crazy," he said. "Just like last time . . . when Marilyn died. Except that he wasn't making any sense! He started screaming that I had stolen some picture from his room." Bernard gestured futilely with his empty hands. "I don't know about any picture! But he went crazy! He kept saying I took it. He threw one of the dog bones through the front window. It smashed into a million pieces. Then he started running through the store, swinging his arms, knocking things down. He even grabbed one of the palm trees and threw it outside. The place looks like a truck drove through it." Bernard clenched his jaw. "And then he grabbed Duke and ran off."

"Duke?" Lily's voice was faint.

Bernard pointed his finger and began to shake his head. "So help me, God, if Nate touches a hair on that monkey's head . . ." Bernard left the sentence unfinished, as he dropped his head into his hands.

Mrs. Hiller sat down next to him, patting him on the back. "He's not going to do anything to Duke, Bernard. We'll find him." She looked at Aunt Wava. "It's been over two hours, now. We've looked all over the neighborhood. The police have put out an all-points bulletin . . ."

Lily didn't wait to hear the end of Mrs. Hiller's sentence. She pushed past Bernard and raced down the steps.

"Lily!" Aunt Wava screamed her name. "Lily, wait!"

But Lily couldn't wait.

She had to find Nate before he hurt Duke.

32

LILY RACED DOWN THE BACK STEPS AND opened the door to Willowood so quickly that she did not even realize Aunt Wava, Bernard, and Mrs. Hiller had followed her.

She strode into the big room with the chandelier and stopped short in front of the fireplace.

The iguana eggs were gone.

"Nate!" she screamed.

There was no answer.

"Lily!" Mrs. Hiller stepped forward, clutching the sides of her cardigan sweater. "Is *this* where you've been spending your time? Down here? In this a*par*tment?" She looked dazed as her eyes roved around the room. "How did you get in? How . . ."

There was no time to explain.

Before Mrs. Hiller could finish her sentence, Lily was off again. She hesitated at the end of the driveway, unsure which direction to run. Where would Nate go if he needed a place to hide? She bolted to the right, deciding to start at the Super Fresh. Maybe Clifford had seen him.

Lily didn't think about how fast she was going or how cold she was without her coat. She didn't notice that most of the yellow and orange leaves above her were turning brown, or that the mannequins in the department store had been changed out of their winter coats and were wearing new glittery dresses and high heels. All she could think about was Nate. And how everything that had happened to him in the last few hours was because of her. How could she have thought that he wouldn't notice the missing picture? She imagined him looking at it every night, the way she did with the picture of her father. How could she have been so stupid?

"Clifford!" she gasped, leaning against the shiny meat case. Clifford was cutting a piece of meat. He grinned when he saw Lily and then put down his knife. "Clifford! Have you seen Nate?"

"Nate?" Clifford frowned and wiped his hands on his white apron. "Not since yesterday."

Lily's heart sank. "He hasn't been in at all today, then?"

Clifford shook his head. "But I'll tell him you're look—"

Lily turned and raced down the slick aisles.

She made a hard left on Main Street, although she wasn't sure where she was going. *Where are you, Nate?* she thought. *Why did you run off? And why did you take the eggs?* Her lungs began to burn as she passed the waterfall, but she kept going, propelled by a fear that swept through her like rushing water. What if he had smashed all the eggs? Something caught in her throat as an image of him stomping on the smooth white shells filled her mind. No, she told herself. Nate wouldn't do that. Not after all he had gone through to get her the eggs in the first place. She wiped her eyes with the back of her hand. But what if he did something to Duke? He had told her straight-out how much he hated the little monkey. What if that was the only way he could think of to get back at his father because he thought that he had stolen the picture?

I don't know if violence ever really leaves a person.

Lily tried to push Mrs. Bing's words out of her head as she rounded the corner of South Main. What she saw then stopped her completely, and she stood there, stunned, gasping for breath. There were three police cars in the middle of the street. Yellow tape had already been strung around the front of Pet Palace and someone in a brown uniform was sweeping the remaining shards of glass off the sidewalk. One policeman was standing next to the store, speaking into a walkie-talkie. Another policeman stood in the middle of the street, directing traffic. People who were trying to get through hung out of their car windows and stared at the mess. Lily couldn't blame them.

The front window of Pet Palace looked like an enormous, punched-in mouth. Through the splintered hole in the window, Lily could see the disarray inside. Boxes and bags were strewn all over the place, and plastic trees had been knocked over. Even the vines along the ceiling had been ripped down and shredded. A parrot was flying loose, swooping back and forth across the store, squawking loudly.

Lily took off again, this time running north. There was no rationale for the direction she chose, but she figured that if she looked long enough, she would run into Nate eventually. As she ran, she tried not to let her thoughts get the best of her, but it was nearly impossible. What if the police found him before she did? What if they arrested him or put him in handcuffs and took him to another special home? She didn't want Nate to go anywhere.

If he went, she decided, she would go with him.

She turned the corner at the end of Pine Avenue and barreled headfirst into a girl who was carrying a shopping bag and drinking an orange soda. The girl screamed as her shopping bag went flying. Her soda spilled all over the front of her shirt. Lily fell to the sidewalk, grabbing her ankle as a fiery pain shot through it.

"You are *so* dead!" a familiar voice said. Lily looked up. Amanda Peterson was holding the front of her wet shirt away from her body and glaring at her. Lily tried to get up, but the pain in her ankle was unbearable. It felt like someone had stuck a scalding knife into it.

"It was an accident!" she said, rolling to one side to try to relieve the pressure on her ankle.

"It was not!" Amanda screamed.

"No." Lily's breath was coming in spurts now as the pain increased. "I . . . swear. I didn't . . . even see . . . you." She tried to get up. Precious minutes that needed to be spent looking for Nate were flying by. But when her foot touched down against the sidewalk, she cried out in pain. There was no way she was going to be able to walk. She looked up at Amanda desperately. "You have to help me! Nate's in trouble!"

Amanda stopped flapping her shirt. She looked at Lily with disgust.

"Nate?" she said. "Retard Nate? You're *still* hanging around with him?"

Lily gritted her teeth.

"What do you mean he's in trouble?" Amanda asked.

Lily took a deep breath. "He ran off. He had a huge fight with his Dad and he took the monkey and no one knows . . ."

She stopped suddenly as she remembered the closet in the back bedroom of Willowood. She had been so alarmed about the missing eggs that she hadn't even thought to look anywhere else in the apartment except the main room.

"What monkey?" Amanda asked. "He has a *monkey*? A real one?"

"Yes," Lily said. "And I'm pretty sure I know where he is. I just have to get to him before anyone else finds him. Amanda, please. You have to help me. I can't walk. Please, help me get up. Please. He has Duke and I don't know what he's going to do . . ."

Lily's sentence trailed off as she realized Amanda was sneering at her.

"You can't be serious," Amanda said. "Do you have *any* idea what kind of trouble I got into with my parents because of you?"

"Because of me?" Lily winced as another stab of pain radiated through her ankle.

"You and Gina Soo," Amanda said. She kicked her empty soda can across the street. "My mother said that if she even hears that I've so much as *looked* at either of you, she'll . . ." Amanda's voice drifted off. The sneer faded from her lips.

Lily remembered what Gina had said about Amanda's parents never being around. Maybe, she thought, Amanda acted the way she did in school because that was the only way she could get her parents to pay any attention to her.

"Listen," she said. "If you help me, I'll talk Gina into letting you win the championship game next week."

Amanda's eyes glittered. "I don't need *your* help to win the championship. I can get that little geek out all by myself."

"You sure?" Lily began to massage her calf. It helped ease the throbbing in her ankle. "Gina's pretty good, you know." She paused. "And she's been practicing." Lily didn't know if Gina had been practicing. But the way Amanda's face blanched when she said it made her realize it was the right thing to say.

Amanda studied Lily on the ground beneath her. She bit the inside of her cheek and ran a finger over her bottom lip.

Then she leaned over and grabbed one of Lily's arms. She hooked it over her shoulders and pulled Lily up. Lily gasped as her ankle burned with pain. Amanda steadied Lily against her hip and then turned her head. Her lips were set in a tight line.

"You tell anyone about this, Sinclair, and you're going to pay for the rest of the year, you got it?"

Lily nodded. "Got it."

33

THE DOOR TO THE CLOSET INSIDE Willowood was closed. It was also locked. From the inside. Lily leaned against Amanda and stared at the heavy glass doorknob, wondering how long Nate had been in there and if he still had Duke with him. Amanda was looking at the door too. Her mouth was hanging open in amazement.

"Where'd you guys find *this* place?" she asked.

Lily put a finger to her lips. "Shhh."

Amanda gave her a dark look. She didn't like being told what to do.

Lily tried to think. If she stood there and yelled for him, Nate would probably refuse to answer. Or he would put her through that "How do I know it's you?" routine he had done in his apartment. She turned to Amanda.

"Listen, I need to talk to him. But it's gotta be done very quietly. I have to lie down and kind of put my mouth against the door."

Amanda reared her head back. "*What?*"

"Will you just help me get down on the ground? Then I can lean over and start talking to him."

"He's *in* there?" she asked, pointing at the door.

"Yeah. Shhhh . . ." Amanda let Lily lean on her as she squatted down on one leg and then brought her injured ankle around in front of her. Lily leaned her cheek against the side of the door and brought her lips close to the white wood.

"Nate!" she whispered. "Nate! It's Lily! Are you okay?" There was no answer, but she could hear Duke's frightened chattering inside. Lily looked up at Amanda, who was sucking on a piece of her hair.

"Is that the monkey?" Amanda whispered.

Lily nodded. She put her cheek against the door again and cleared her throat. This time she talked slightly louder.

"Nate! Your dad came over to my apartment a little while ago. He told me what happened." She paused. "And I want you to know it's not your fault. It's mine. I want to tell you about it. Can you open the door?"

Silence.

Lily looked up again. There was no way she was going to go into all of this in front of Amanda Peterson, no matter how nice she had just been.

"Listen," Lily said. "I have to tell him something kind of personal. Would you mind sitting over there"—she pointed through the bedroom door into the wide front room—"just until I'm done?" Lily held her breath, waiting for Amanda to kick her in the face. Instead, Amanda turned and walked through the door and into the front room. She sat down next to the black fireplace and hugged her knees into her chest.

"Nate," Lily tried again. "Please open the door. I have to tell you something." Nothing.

"Nate, I'm the one who took your mom's picture. I wanted to—" Lily stopped talking as the door began to open slowly. Nate peeked out. His eyes were puffy around the edges and his face was wet. His red hat was snapped tightly around his chin.

"*You* took Mama's picture?"

"I wanted . . . I wanted to make you a better one," Lily said. "As a present. My Aunt Wava was going to draw you a bigger one."

"I want it back," Nate said, stretching out his arm. "Give it."

"I can't," Lily said. "It's upstairs in my apartment. And I hurt my . . ." Nate began to close the door. "Wait!" Lily said, grabbing the door. "What are you doing? Come out, Nate. You can help me upstairs and we'll go get it now."

"You're lying," Nate said. "Pop took it."

"No, he didn't! I did! I told you, I wanted to make you a bigger one. I didn't mean to steal it, Nate! I just meant to borrow it. I was gonna—"

"I hate Pop!" Nate yelled. "I hate his guts!"

"Don't!" Lily was frustrated. "He didn't take the picture, Nate. *I* did, I already told you. You should be mad at me."

"I hate his guts," Nate said again, shaking his head. "He only loves Duke."

"No he doesn't. He loves you, too."

"No!" Nate screamed. "He hates me! He told me. He hates my guts. He told me I'm *crazy*!" He clenched his fists and squeezed his eyes as he screamed the last word. Lily sat back, frightened. Out of the corner of her eye, she saw Amanda get up and run out the back door. Mrs. Bing's warning reverberated in the back of her head again. Was Nate going to lose it, the way he had just a few hours ago in the store? Was she safe? With her ankle, she couldn't abandon him even if she wanted to. But, she realized suddenly, she didn't want to.

"He said I'm crazy!" Nate sobbed. "Crazy!"

"Since when is it a bad thing to be crazy?" Lily asked, thinking quickly.

Nate wiped his face with the back of a dirty hand. "What?"

"We're all crazy. Remember? That's what the Cheshire cat said. He told Alice that everyone was crazy. Even him."

"He said we were all *mad*," Nate corrected softly.

"Which means crazy, right?" Lily asked.

Nate looked at her suspiciously.

"So if your dad thinks you're mad, then I am too. And so is he."

Nate picked the chipped paint off the side of the closet door.

"Just like the Cheshire cat said," Lily finished softly.

Nate scratched his nose. "I have Beatrice's eggs," he said.

"You do?" Lily tried not to sound too excited. "In there?"

"Yeah. It's freezing in this apartment, Lily. They're not gonna hatch if they get too cold."

"Is it too late?" Lily asked.

"I don't think so." Nate licked his lips. "We gotta get 'em warm, though."

A sudden, frantic scratching sounded from inside the closet.

"Is that Duke?" Lily asked.

Nate nodded.

"Is he . . . okay?"

"Who cares?" Nate asked. His voice was hard again.

"Me," Lily said in a little voice. "I care about Duke. And I care about you, Nate. I want you to be okay."

"I miss Mama," Nate said, his voice cracking. "It's all my fault she's gone."

"Nate," Lily started. "It's not your—"

"Yes!" Nate roared. "It is! We got into a big fight the day she died. I yelled at her and told her she stunk! And right after I said that, she grabbed onto the side of the kitchen chair, and her eyes got all big, and then . . . she fell." Nate squeezed his eyes shut. "And she didn't get up again, no matter how much I begged and cried. She wouldn't get up!"

"But that doesn't mean you did it!" Lily cried. "She just . . . her heart . . . it was weak, right? It just—"

"Pop said I broke her heart." Nate said each word so loudly that Lily sat back, frightened. "Me!" Nate stabbed at the front of his shirt with his index finger. "I *broke* it! *I* did it!"

Lily stared at Nate for a moment. She thought about all

the reasons Mom had given her about her missing father, and how she had never been able to accept any of them. They weren't enough. And the reason they weren't enough was because none of them had answered the real question that she had been carrying inside all this time.

Duke appeared suddenly, peeking out from behind Nate's red hat like a stuffed animal. He was wearing a yellow sweater and eating a piece of salami in tiny, rapid bites. Lily wanted to jump up and kiss him. But the sound of footsteps made her turn around. They got louder as they moved through the front room, followed by the sound of frantic voices. "Lily! Nate!"

"Over here!" It was Amanda's voice. "They're over here."

Mom and Aunt Wava and Bernard and Mrs. Hiller all came rushing into the room. "Lily!" Mom cried, sinking to her knees.

Nate shoved Duke toward Lily, ducked back into the closet, and slammed the door shut. Lily could hear the lock click from the inside. "Oh, honey," Mom said. "Oh, my goodness, I was so worried! Are you okay?"

"Duke!" Bernard hollered. The little monkey rushed over and sprang into Bernard's arms. Bernard made a sound like a sob had gotten caught in his throat. For a split second, Lily wondered if what Nate had said about his father were true. Did he love Duke more than him?

Mom began patting Lily's legs. "Which foot is it, Lily? What can—"

"Don't touch it!" Lily screamed. "Please! It hurts!"

Mom looked over at Aunt Wava. "Call an ambulance. It's turning blue. I think it might be broken."

Aunt Wava began to run. Then she turned and rushed back over toward Lily. "Here." She pushed the photograph of Nate's mother into Lily's hand. "I thought you might need this."

"Where's Nate?" Bernard asked. He looked around the room stupidly, still nuzzling Duke with his nose.

"He's in there," Lily said, pointing to the closet. "And he's not coming out."

"That's what *he* thinks." Bernard's voice was tight. He went over to the door and rapped on it sharply with the backs of his knuckles. "Nathaniel! It's Pop! You come outta there right now, you hear?"

"He's not *coming* out," Lily said.

"Lily," Mom whispered. "Don't interfere."

Lily ignored her. "He's not gonna come out until you tell him the truth."

"The truth?" Bernard repeated. "About what?"

"About his mother." Lily struggled up onto her good leg, using Mom's shoulder for support. "You tell him the truth,

Bernard." Her voice was quavering. She had never spoken to an adult like this and it made her nervous. Bernard had done so much for her by giving her a job in the store and introducing her to all his lizards. But this wasn't about any of those things. This was about trying to make things right for Nate.

"I don't know what you're talking about," Bernard said. "And I don't think I like your tone of voice either."

Mom rubbed Lily's fingers, which were still gripping her shoulder. "Honey, sit down. Let Bernard handle this with Nate his way."

"His way doesn't work," Lily said. "You guys think that because you're adults you have all the answers. But you don't."

"I still don't . . ." Bernard started, scratching his head.

"You told Nate that it was his fault his mother died," Lily said, trying to stop the wobbly way the words were coming out of her mouth.

"I did no such thing!" Bernard looked outraged. "And you have no right—"

"You did!" Lily burst out. "You told him he broke her heart!"

Bernard's face went pale. "He thinks . . ." He staggered back a few steps. "Oh my God, of course he does." He stood there for a few seconds, staring at Lily over the tips of his fingers, which were cupped around his mouth.

"Just tell him the truth," Lily said. She held out the photograph. Her hand was shaking.

Bernard stared at Lily for a moment, as if trying to figure out what she had just said. Then he crept over to the closet door and knocked gently on it. "Nate?" His voice was hoarse. "Nate, it's Pop. I need to talk to you."

"Beat it!" Nate hollered from inside the closet. "I don't want to talk to you! Ever!"

"No, Nate." Bernard tapped on the door again, a little more softly. "Open the door, son. Please. Pop needs to explain something to you."

Two guys in T-shirts and white pants came in the room suddenly. One of them was carrying a big bag. Aunt Wava was behind them.

"You the one who hurt your ankle?" the guy with the bag asked.

Lily looked over her shoulder as the men lifted her up and carried her out of the room.

Amanda had disappeared completely.

But Nate had opened the door a crack.

34

IT TURNED OUT THAT LILY'S ANKLE wasn't broken after all, just sprained. But it swelled up to the size of a grapefruit and turned purple. The doctor wrapped it tightly in an ACE bandage and told Mom to ice it every four hours. Lily thought it looked like a funny little armadillo under the brown bandage, with just her toes sticking out of one end. It still hurt.

Mom set her up on the couch and arranged three pillows under her ankle. She brought Weemis in and set his cage on the floor next to the couch. Mrs. Hiller made Lily a cup of coffee in her favorite gecko mug and brought in a plate of sliced apples and orange sections. She sat down in the easy chair across from the couch.

"Where's Nate?" Lily asked, taking a piece of apple and nibbling it around the edge.

"He's back home with Bernard," Mrs. Hiller said softly. "They're cleaning up. Everything's fine." She gave Lily the kind of smile that was more than just a smile; it was a look that said she understood Lily in a way she hadn't before.

Lily smiled back.

"Well," Aunt Wava said from across the room. "This is a visit *I'll* never forget."

"Do you really have to go?" Lily asked.

Aunt Wava nodded. "My bus leaves in an hour, pumpkin. But I finished the picture for you while you were at the emergency room." Lily sat up as best as she could. Aunt Wava brought it into the living room and held it up in front of her chest. "Ta-da!"

Mrs. Hiller made a small squeaking sound and then clapped her hand over her mouth. "Oh!" she said. "It looks exactly like Marilyn!"

Lily stared. It was the most beautiful picture she had ever seen. Aunt Wava had painted Nate's mother in the softest of colors: her face was a muted pale peach, her eyes blue, the sweater around her shoulders lemon yellow, and her lips light rose. She looked radiant, as if a candle was being held behind the canvas, giving it a delicate glow.

"He'll love it, Aunt Wava!" she said. "Thank you so much!"

Aunt Wava hugged her hard and sat down on the couch. "I'm glad I could help out. You take care of that ankle, okay? I want you in good shape when you come down next month to see the show."

"Don't worry," Lily said. "I'll be ready."

She leaned in close as Aunt Wava held her again. "I love you, Lily. I love everything about you."

Lily smiled. She lifted her face. "Mugga-mugga?"

Aunt Wava leaned in.

This time, Lily couldn't feel the ring at all in the side of her nose.

"Mom?" Lily called from her seat on the couch.

Mom emerged from the kitchen, wiping a glass with a dish towel. "Yes, babes?"

Lily patted a space next to her. "Can we talk for a minute?"

Mom put the glass down slowly and walked over to the couch. She had a concerned look on her face. "Everything all right?"

Lily took a deep breath. "I need to ask you something," she said. "It's something I've asked you about a few times before and you've never really answered me."

Mom looked perplexed. She leaned over and tucked a piece of hair behind Lily's shoulder. "What is it, love?"

"I don't want you to get mad." Lily hesitated. "I just . . . I just really need you to tell me the truth. I need you to give me a real answer. Something that . . ."

"Lily." Her mother was looking at her head-on. "Honey. Whatever it is, I will do my best to give you what you need. Okay? Go ahead."

"Okay." Lily smoothed the blanket over her thighs. She swallowed. "Why did my dad leave me?" She was surprised at how steady her voice was. "Why, Mom?"

Mom licked her lips. She stared at the floor for a moment as if the answer she needed might be down around her feet somewhere. Then she inhaled and looked at Lily. "You know why he left, Lily? He left because he was scared."

Lily frowned. "Of what?"

"Of being an adult. Of having you. He was only twenty when you were born. I know that seems old to you, but it's really not. You wait and see."

"Were *you* scared?"

Mom laughed. "Terrified. I was only nineteen when I had you. When the nurses in the hospital wrapped you up and gave you to me, I couldn't believe they were really going to let me take you home. I didn't know anything about babies."

"But you learned."

Mom smiled. "And I'm still learning. I learn new things about you every day."

Lily scowled. "So my dad just didn't want to grow up?"

"I don't think he wanted all the responsibilities that come with *being* grown-up," Mom said. "You know, having to support a family, taking care of a little baby. I think it just frightened him too much. So he ran."

Lily tilted her head so that she was looking straight at Mom. "You don't think it was because I made too much noise? As a baby, I mean? Or that I was too—"

Mom cut Lily off with a hug so tight that for a moment, Lily couldn't breathe. "No, no, no, no, no, no, no, no!" she said over Lily's shoulder. "Not ever, sweetie! Nothing you did made him leave." She drew back, cupping Lily's face with both hands. "Look at me, sweetheart." Lily stared into Mom's eyes. For the first time, she saw tiny flecks of gold swimming around in all that blue. "*None* of this is your fault, Lily. Do you understand me? Your father made a choice that was about him. It had nothing to do with you. Nothing. Okay?"

Lily tried to nod, but Mom's hands were squeezing her face so tightly, she couldn't move. "Mom."

Mom looked at her breathlessly. "Yes, sweetie?"

"I can't breathe. Let go."

Mom released her hands, giggling a little. "Oh, angel," she said. "I love you so much. I'm so sorry you have been carrying this around for so long. I don't know why I didn't figure it out."

"It's all right," Lily said, rubbing her cheeks. "Really, it is."

"No, it's not." Mom was shaking her head. "I should've been as honest with you as I could—right from the beginning. I guess I've been so mad at him all these years that that was the only thing I ever thought about." She lightly ran her finger down Lily's cheek. "I'll make it up to you, sweetie. I don't know how yet, but I will. I promise."

Lily bit the inside of her cheek. "I know how you can make it up to me."

"How?"

"You can quit smoking," Lily said. "For good."

Mom nodded her head slowly. "Okay." The tone in her voice was final, as if maybe for the first time, she really believed she could do it. "You got it, Lily."

35

LATER THAT AFTERNOON, LILY ASKED Mom to drop her off at the Doughn't You Know It bakery downtown. She had to talk to Gina, and she didn't want to wait until Monday to do it, since Monday was also the day of the championship dodgeball game. Mom was worried, since Lily was still having trouble on her crutches, but Lily assured her she would be fine.

The inside of the bakery smelled like fresh bread, vanilla frosting, and baked apples. Long, narrow loaves of bread were stacked on a table right by the door. Another table was covered with fat, short loaves, dusted with flour. Lily made her way over to an enormous glass case in the middle of the store. The right-hand side of the glass case was filled with cakes. Some had chocolate frosting, others had pink frosting; there were even a few with blue frosting. Next to the cakes were all the different cookies that Gina brought to lunch every day. They were lined neatly in rows, with small white cards in front that identified them.

There was also a man behind the counter. He was Asian like Gina, and very short. His dark hair was parted on one side and he had on a pair of black glasses.

"Hey there!" he said when he saw Lily. "What can I do for you today?"

"I'm a friend of Gina's," Lily said. "From school. Is she here?"

The man lifted a finger. "Your name wouldn't be Lily, would it?"

Lily looked at him in surprise. "Yeah! That is my name."

The man extended his arm over the counter so that Lily could shake his hand. "Well, it's an honor to finally meet you, Lily. I'm Mr. Soo. The way Gina talks about you every day, I knew I'd meet you sooner or later."

"Gina talks about me?"

"Oh, does she!" Mr. Soo slapped his chest with his hands. A puff of flour floated into the air around him. "Every night at dinner! She says you're one of the nicest girls she's ever met." Lily looked at the floor and squirmed a little. Gina wasn't going to think she was so nice when she asked her the favor.

Gina came in from the back just then, holding a giant tray of coconut cookies. "Where do you want these, Daddy?"

Mr. Soo pointed to an empty space inside the glass case. "Right there, Gina. Next to the pistachio crescents."

Gina slid the tray inside the case and then caught a glimpse of Lily. "Hey, Lily! What are you doing here? Why are you on crutches?"

"It's a long story," Lily said, hobbling forward again. "I . . . uh . . . wanted to see your place. And I kind of . . . um . . . needed to talk to you." Gina slid the back of the glass case shut and came out around the front of it. She had flour all over the front of her jeans and along the arms of her shirt.

"Is everything okay?"

Lily shrugged. "Sorta." She glanced at Mr. Soo.

Gina pushed her glasses up along her nose and turned around. "We're gonna go in the back, Daddy. Just for a few minutes."

Mr. Soo nodded. "Take your time," he said. "When you're done, you can come back out for a slice of chocolate cheesecake."

Gina led Lily into the kitchen. It wasn't very big. In fact, the stainless-steel table in the middle of it, which was covered with trays of baked goods, took up most of the space. Long ovens lined the far wall and next to them were shelves of bread wrapped in plastic bags. Gina pulled up two stools alongside the table and helped Lily get on hers.

"Okay," Gina said, straddling her own stool. "So what's up?"

Lily plunged in, starting at the very beginning. Gina's forehead creased into a map of tiny lines as Lily relayed how she had run through the city, looking desperately for Nate and how she had accidentally run smack into Amanda.

"A*man*da?" Gina repeated. "Geez, of all people."

"That's not even the worst part," Lily said grimly.

"She kicked you?" Gina guessed, looking down at Lily's bandaged foot.

Lily shook her head. "My foot was already hurt. I couldn't stand. I begged Amanda to help me find Nate, but she wouldn't." Lily hung her head. "I did something terrible, Gina. I'm so sorry."

"What?"

"I told Amanda that if she helped me, I'd talk you into losing the championship."

Gina looked confused for a moment. "The dodgeball championship?" she said finally.

Lily nodded her head. "I know I shouldn't have. I had no right to do something like that, Gina. I was just . . . so panicky. It was the only thing I could think of."

Gina slowly got off her stool. She crossed her arms and stuck out her lower lip. "After all that girl has done to me—to *us,* Lily—you want me to just hand her the *championship*?" Her voice was dangerously quiet.

Lily stared at the floor. Her face was hot with shame.

"Get out," Gina said.

Lily looked up, shocked.

"I mean it," Gina said. "Leave. Now." She pointed toward the front door with her finger.

"Gina . . . I . . ."

Lily stopped as Gina began walking toward the back of the kitchen. "Don't," she said without turning around. "Because I'm not listening to another word you ever have to say again."

36

LILY DIDN'T SLEEP AT ALL THAT NIGHT. She stared at her glow-in-the-dark stars on the ceiling and adjusted the pillow under her ankle at least a hundred times. Weemis was busy scurrying around in his cage, but Lily talked to him anyway, even though he didn't get up on his rock and look at her even once. She had left the bakery soon after her conversation with Gina, politely refusing the cheesecake Mr. Soo had tried to get her to take with her. She had already taken enough from Gina, she thought.

How in the world had she managed to mess things up so badly? Not only was she going to have to continue to deal with Amanda for the rest of the year, but now she wouldn't even have Gina to talk to. Tears rolled down the sides of her face as she realized how much she would miss her. Gina was her friend. A real one, like Bailey had been. And she had gone and thrown it all away by doing something stupid.

She buried her face in her pillow and held her breath, hoping that it would ease the ache in the middle of her chest.

It ached even more.

She tried to think about the eggs instead. Nate had them somewhere safe, somewhere warm. In less than a month, if the baby iguanas were still growing inside those small, rubbery shells, they would be here. She thought she would give anything right now to have a shell of some kind around her, something she could crawl inside and not come back out of until she was ready.

Lily's stomach plummeted as she made her way down the fifth-floor hallway Monday morning and saw Amanda standing next to her locker. She couldn't imagine what Amanda had to say to her, but as her head started spinning, she saw Amanda stick a folded-up piece of paper into the slot at the top of her locker and then walk away. Lily hobbled forward slowly. She didn't want to see what was on the paper. After everything Amanda had witnessed over the weekend, who knew what awful thing she had written about her and Nate this time?

She slowly opened her locker. The square of paper drifted out, floating to the floor like a little butterfly. Lily picked up the note and unfolded it. The chunky, curly script said:

Lily-

Don't ask Gina to lose the game.

She doesn't need to do that for you or for me.

Amanda

P.S. Gina and Nate are lucky to have you as a friend.

Gina wouldn't turn around in homeroom, not even when Lily tapped on her shoulder. Lily tried again. And then another time. But Gina wouldn't budge. Lily gave up after Mrs. Bing yelled at everyone to sit down. But when her teacher turned around for a moment to write something on the board, Lily dropped Amanda's note over Gina's shoulder. She held her breath as it fell into Gina's lap, hoping that she wouldn't toss it back without reading it.

Gina didn't toss it back in Lily's direction. But she

let it sit there for a while. She didn't move a muscle as Mrs. Bing reviewed vocabulary words, went over social studies terms from the glossary in the textbook and discussed the many inventions of Thomas Edison. It wasn't until Mrs. Bing told everyone to get out their reading books and read quietly to themselves that Gina looked down at the note. Lily watched for some sort of indication that Gina was reading it, but minutes passed and Gina did not move. After another moment or so, Gina folded the note back up. She lifted it carefully and, without turning around, let the note fall with a plop in the middle of Lily's desk.

The gymnasium was abuzz with excitement. The entire fifth grade—except for Amanda and Gina, who were waiting in the locker rooms, and Lily, who was sitting on the benches because of her ankle—were in a circle, pounding the floor with their shoes. Stomp, stomp, *stomp!* Stomp, stomp, *stomp*! Lily could not pound anything with her bad foot, but she doubted she would have anyway, with Gina still refusing to acknowledge her.

Mr. Finkelsteiner strode out into the middle of the floor. He blew his whistle and lifted his arm, putting an end to all the noise. "This is it, guys!" he yelled. "After two weeks of intense semifinal eliminations, the field has been narrowed down to two final contenders!" He blew his whistle and Amanda and Gina came running out. The students went crazy at the sight of the girls, pounding the air with their fists. Lily tried not to shudder as she thought about how ferocious the game had become. Every single student standing in the circle was going to try his or her hardest to get Gina or Amanda out. How could Gina stand it? The pressure was mind-boggling.

Lily tried to get a read on what Gina was thinking, but Gina's face was set like stone. She seemed oblivious to the screams around her, as if she were in a bubble. She was going to give this 100 percent, Lily realized, even if the odds and the crowd were against her. She wasn't a quitter. No matter what. Lily knew that Gina didn't want to be her friend anymore, but for a moment, she didn't care. She was proud of her anyway. Gina was fierce. She was brave, like Alice.

"Let's go, Gina!" she screamed. "You can do it!" Her voice rang, unashamed and lonely, throughout the gym. The other students stared at her. Gina did not even blink.

Gina and Amanda strode to the center of the circle. Mr. Finkelsteiner handed the ball to Margaret Haggerson, who was closest to him. He blew his whistle. The game began.

After the first few throws, it was clear that neither girl was going to go down without a fight. Both of them were at the top of their game, exerting every last bit of effort into each movement they made. The ball flew back and forth at least forty times, missing ankles and feet and knees and calves by a hair's breadth. Once, as Clive's ball shot into the circle, Gina misjudged its direction and arched her back at the last possible second. The ball missed her by a quarter of an inch. It went spinning into the opposite corner and bounced off the wall. Clive started to curse—and then stopped himself, clapping his palm over his mouth. Mr. Finkelsteiner gave him a nod.

After twenty minutes, Gina's face was bright pink. Her neck was nearly the same color as her glasses. Lily noticed that Gina's arms were trembling, and when she pushed her glasses up her nose, her hands shook. Amanda was breathing hard too. After every throw, she would lean over and rest her palms on her knees. But both girls' eyes blazed with a doggedness that kept them upright despite their exhaustion.

It was Owen's turn to throw. He paced up and down the floor, snarling like a tiger. The ball rested lightly on his fingertips. On either side of him, the rest of the kids screamed and jumped up and down. They knew, just as Lily did, that Owen's throw was personal; he was going to get back at Gina for getting him out in the semifinals. Gina stood still in the middle of the circle, watching Owen carefully. Mr. Finkelsteiner blew his whistle, indicating that Owen's time to throw was running out. Owen tossed the ball up into the air casually. Then he caught it and fired.

Lily watched Gina as the ball hurtled toward her. She seemed confused for a split second as her glasses slid further down her nose. The ball swung wide and then, like a small planet on its own orbit, spun wildly toward her feet. She leapt into the air, but not fast enough. The ball clipped her on the heel and, amid a shout from the sidelines, the game was over.

Mr. Finkelsteiner's whistle shrieked. "Peterson takes it!" The students rushed from the bench, lifting Amanda to their shoulders and screaming her name.

Grabbing her crutches, Lily hobbled awkwardly across the floor until she reached Gina. "Gina!" Gina was lying flat on her back, staring up at the ceiling. "Gina, you okay?"

Gina sat up. "Yeah." She was breathing hard. "I'm okay."

Lily sat next to her. "Did you . . ." She paused, unsure if she should say it.

"Let her win?" Gina finished.

Lily nodded.

"Not on your life."

Lily grinned.

They sat there for a few seconds, watching the melee around them. Lily turned back toward Gina. "You still mad?" she asked.

Gina nodded. She stared directly at Lily. "That was a rotten thing to do to a friend."

Lily swallowed. "I know. I'm sorry." She looked at Gina and for a split second, she could see the hurt in her eyes. "I'll never do something like that again, Gina. I promise."

Gina nodded slowly.

Mr. Finkelsteiner's whistle shrieked behind them. "Showers, gang! And next week, we're playing lightning tag! Amanda's pick!"

"Oh, man." Gina got to her feet slowly. "Figures Amanda would pick another contact sport."

"Too bad you can't sit on the sidelines," Lily said, resting her armpits over the tops of her crutches. "With me."

Gina raised her eyebrows. "You kidding? I gotta beat Amanda this time."

Lily laughed.

Gina threw her arm over her shoulder.

"You're all sweaty," Lily said.

"Too bad," Gina said. "That's what happens when you play real dodgeball."

37

AUNT WAVA WAS FOREVER TELLING LILY that New York City was the best city in the world, and as Lily walked out from the bus terminal onto Forty-second Street, she understood why. She laughed to herself as she remembered thinking Riverside Heights was such a big city. New York City was like a whole separate country! There were skyscrapers so high, it looked like they were making holes in the clouds. And some of the buildings had gigantic pictures of people in their underwear on the sides of them. The streets had hundreds of stores, and whenever she turned a corner, there was always a hot dog or pretzel stand sitting there, as if it were waiting just for her.

Aunt Wava showed them how to step into the middle of the street and whistle for a cab through their fingers. Lily climbed inside when one pulled over and tried to look at the tops of the buildings, pressing her face so hard against the window that she could feel her teeth against her cheek.

"Hey! I can't see!"

She moved over to let Nate in. He craned his neck and looked out the window. "They're too high," he said in disgust.

Bernard, who was sitting in the front seat with the cab driver, guffawed. "That's why they're called *sky*scrapers, you big lunk." Mom, who was sitting next to Aunt Wava on the other side of Nate, laughed and patted his hand.

Having Nate and Bernard come with them to New York had happened at the last minute. Aunt Wava, who was getting more and more nervous about her show, called two days earlier and told Mom that she needed one more portrait to round out her show. She didn't have time, she said, to start another one from scratch. Could they possibly bring the one she had done of Nate's mother?

Bernard didn't hesitate. "I'll do you one better," he said. "Nate and I have never been to the Big Apple. How would you feel about us joining you?" He looked over at Nate. "That is, if you want to loan Aunt Wava your picture, Nate." Lily's heart raced as she waited for Nate to answer. She stared hard at him, trying to tell him with her eyes how much she wanted him to come.

"I get it back, right?" Nate asked Mom. "'Cause I need it back."

Mom smiled. "Absolutely, Nate. That one's yours to keep."

Lily grabbed Nate's hand and jumped up and down. "We'll get to see the *Alice in Wonderland* statue!" she screamed. "You and me together!"

Now she looked back out the window and watched more people on the street. It seemed to her that everyone was in a hurry. They either ran or walked so fast that they could hardly breathe. The taxi stopped suddenly at a red light.

"Looka them dogs," Bernard said. Lily looked out the front window. A tall man, wearing a bright orange coat and black gloves, was walking six or seven dogs. They pulled on their leashes, drooling and panting in the cold, getting ready to run. "I don't know 'bout keeping dogs cooped up in the city," Bernard said. "They need to run."

"Oh, they'll run in the park," Aunt Wava said. "They love the park." She sat forward and squeezed Bernard's shoulder. "You miss Duke?"

Lily bit the inside of her cheek. Aunt Wava didn't know anything about the history of Duke and Nate and Bernard. Still, she wished she would stop talking.

"Nah," Bernard said. "What am I gonna do with a

monkey on a trip to New York City? He's fine."

Lily watched out of the corner of her eye as Nate sat back against the black seat and sighed contentedly.

Central Park was an icy wonderland. It had rained and then frozen over the night before, leaving everything in the park still and shiny and silent. The tree branches looked as if someone had rubbed Vaseline all over them and the dark road that wound in and around the park was wet and glistening. Even the grass was brushed with a white coat of frost. People appeared sporadically, like afterthoughts. Joggers wearing earmuffs and thick hats ran along the paths. Their breath came out of their mouths in little clouds, and their cheeks were red from the cold. A man and woman wearing heavy fur coats walked by, arm in arm. Every time the woman's yellow heels slid on the small patches of ice, she made little shrieking noises. The man held her tightly and laughed.

Aunt Wava waved and pointed. "Alice is right around the corner," she said. "Whenever you're ready."

Nate and Lily looked at each other for a split second and then tore off in the direction Aunt Wava had pointed. They stopped as they turned the corner. The only sound was the rise and fall of their panting and the crunch of frost beneath their feet. Alice, glossy with ice, sat before them like a dream. One of her hands was extended, offering them a cup of tea. Her long hair, held back with her signature headband, cascaded over one of her shoulders. A tiny chipmunk sat nibbling an acorn in the small nest of her lap. On her right was the Mad Hatter, sitting lightly on a mushroom cap. He was leaning forward, as if he were trying to talk to her. The March Hare was on her left, holding a large stopwatch.

"Look!" Nate said, walking closer to it. "Behind her elbow!" Lily looked. There was the Cheshire cat, sitting on a little bush behind Alice's left ear.

"They're all here," Nate whispered, sinking down to the ground. "All of 'em. Right here. For real."

Out of nowhere, it began to snow. Tiny little sugar flakes fell out of the sky and clung to Lily's hair and the arms of her coat. She breathed in and out, watching her breath curl up and then disappear in front of her.

If she lived in New York City, she thought, this would be her Willowood.

It was perfect.

38

IT WAS A FEW WEEKS AFTER CHRISTMAS. The sky was a soft white, like cotton. A snow sky, Mrs. Hiller called it. Lily hoped she was right. They hadn't had a real snowfall since the light dusting in Central Park, and she wanted to go sledding with Nate and Gina. Nate had told her about a hill behind the Super Fresh that all the kids used. It sounded amazing.

Mrs. Hiller put the phone down as Lily dropped her backpack on the floor and shut the door.

"Hello, dear. Pick up your backpack, please."

Lily picked it back up. "Who was on the phone?"

"Nate," Mrs. Hiller replied. "He said to tell you to come down to the store as soon as you can."

"But I don't have to be there until four," Lily said.

Mrs. Hiller smiled. "The eggs are hatching," she whispered.

Lily's mouth dropped open. Then she screamed. It was a loud, piercing sound that reverberated through the apartment like an alarm. Mrs. Hiller clapped her hands over her ears and laughed. "Let's go! Let's go!" Lily jumped up and down, pulling on Mrs. Hiller's hand. "Come on, hurry! I don't want to miss it!"

Bernard and Nate were both standing over the incubator when Lily and Mrs. Hiller arrived. Since the ordeal at Willowood, Nate had taken the eggs back to the store. Bernard had helped him redeposit the eggs in a large basin filled with the dirt mixture and put it under a heating lamp so that the babies could warm up again—and stay warm. Still, Bernard had warned Lily that the eggs would probably not hatch. Even under the best of circumstances, most iguana eggs did not hatch in captivity and these eggs had been in the cold for far too long.

Now, Lily watched anxiously as Bernard gently poked at the dirt mixture with his index finger. He had a grim look on his face. Duke peered over his left shoulder, quietly chewing an oyster cracker.

"Are we too late?" Lily cried, rushing up beside Nate. "Did we miss it?"

Bernard dug his whole hand under two of the eggs and lifted them out of the dirt. "Lily, sweetheart," he said. "These guys didn't make it." He rolled the eggs over in the center of his palm and pointed to a weird, fuzzy growth on the shell. "That's fungus," he said. "When eggs get that, it means that the babies are already dead." Lily opened her mouth. Nothing came out but a squeaking sound.

Nate yanked her elbow. "But look," he whispered, pointing to the opposite end of the basin. "Look at that one."

Lily stared as the leathery shell, already split down the middle, moved a fraction of an inch. The shell was white, which made it easy to see the dark creature inside of it. Lily held her breath as the split widened again.

"Oh!" Mrs. Hiller peeped.

A tiny nostril appeared at the opening, followed by the rest of the baby iguana's nose. In a few more minutes, the animal had wriggled its head out, exposing its eyes—which were sealed shut—and brown, wrinkly neck. It was the most adorable thing Lily had ever seen. Lily looked up for a split second. Mrs. Hiller, Bernard, Duke, and Nate were all watching her. Their faces were glowing. She thought for a second that if she could look inside, she would probably be glowing too.

"He's gonna be fine," Bernard said. "You're gonna be able to take him home tomorrow."

"What're you gonna name him?" Nate asked.

Lily grinned so hard that her cheeks hurt.

"What?" Nate pushed. "Some girly name, right? Like Rosey?"

Lily shook her head.

"Then what?"

Lily was so happy that she laughed out loud. "Superman!" she shouted. "Isn't that perfect?"

A slow smile spread across Nate's face. "Yeah," he said. "That rocks."

39

LILY LAY IN BED FOR A LONG TIME THAT night, thinking about everything that had gone on over the past few weeks. For some reason, she wanted to write it down. She pulled out the paragraph Mrs. Bing had had them write a few days earlier.

What is the most distinctive thing about you?

And if you could change it, would you?

She reread what she had written, and then crumpled it up into a ball. Taking out a fresh piece of paper from her notebook, she lay her head back against the pillow and stared up at the ceiling. After a while, she picked up her pencil and began to write:

The most distinctive thing about me is my family.

She stopped. Her thoughts were racing. She began to say them aloud as they came into her head, the way Gina had told her to do, and then to write. She couldn't believe it. It was actually working! She kept going.

> *The reason it's unique is because it's not your usual kind of family. I don't have a mom and dad and a dog and a house the way lots of kids I know do. I have a mom, who's one of the coolest people on the planet and who I love more than anything, even if she does have to work a lot. I have my pet gecko, Weemis, who listens to everything I say. My Aunt Wava, who's an artist and drew me my very own portrait. Bernard and Nate let me help out at the pet store and make me laugh, and Gina, who will probably be one of my best friends forever, has taught me how to be a real friend. And I have Mrs. Hiller, who's kind of old but who takes good care of me when Mom's not here, even if she is vegetable-happy.*

Lily stopped and thought for a minute. She chewed on the end of her pencil. Then she picked it up and began to write again.

I used to think that I would change all of this if I could. I mean, whoever heard of a family with a mom, a gecko, an aunt, three friends, and an old lady??? I never have. But now I know I wouldn't change any of it. Not one single thing. My family is unique, which means that it is one of a kind. And that means that I'm one of the luckiest people I know.

She read it out loud to herself when she had finished, and put it under her pillow.

Then she took the picture of her father and placed it deep in the bottom of her top drawer, under all her winter socks.

Here's a sneak peek at
the latest book
from Cecilia Galante:

I thought it was funny.

So did a lot of other kids.

Miss Movado, however, did not.

Neither did Mr. Pringle, the middle school principal. Mr. Pringle used to be a drill sergeant in the army. With his shaved head and starched shirts, he still looks like one. He glared at me now above his steepled fingers, waiting, I guess, for me to burst into tears and admit that I was responsible. Instead I stared at the mounted fish that hung on the wall behind his head. Its silvery scales had been painted a dark blue on the bottom and a nose, sharp as a needle, stuck out of the front of it. I wondered if deep down, Mr. Pringle wished he could do the same thing to some of his students that he'd done to that fish.

"Maeve," Mr. Pringle said sternly. "Look at me."

I bristled. "It's *May*. Not Maeve."

"May." Mr. Pringle stood up, leaning his whole weight on just the tips of his fingers until they turned white. "Look at me." I glanced over at him. A tiny bead of sweat was balanced on his upper lip. "We know it was you. Pete *saw* you in her room with the spray-paint can."

Pete was the school janitor. I'd seen the top of his bald head go by through the little square hole in Miss Movado's door just as I was finishing up, and jumped so fast into the coat closet that I almost fell over. It was a tiny, airless space. One of Miss Movado's hideous cardigan sweaters was hanging behind me. I waited, inhaling the scent of butterscotch and her too-sweet perfume, until I thought I might get sick. Ten minutes went by, but Pete did not return. Finally I slipped back out, grabbed the can of spray paint, and ran. It hadn't even occurred to me that he might have seen me.

I shifted in my chair. The back of my legs made a peeling sound against the red leather. "Pete couldn't have seen me," I said. "Because I wasn't *there*."

Mr. Pringle studied me for a moment, as if examining a new specimen of fish. How long had that poor fish struggled? I wondered, glancing up at it once more. How hard had Mr. Pringle pulled and reeled his line until, exhausted, the poor thing had given up? Probably pretty long. Well, he wasn't going to reel *me* in, no matter how hard he pulled or how long he tried.

"We have *video* of you in the hallway too, Maeve. Right outside Miss Movado's classroom. Just you. No one else."

My cheeks flushed hot. I'd forgotten about the school cameras. "It must've been someone else. Someone who looks like me."

Mr. Pringle shook his head as he came around to the front of his desk. Leaning back against the smooth wood, he crossed his arms over his red tie. A gold wedding ring peeked out from the finger on his left hand. "You're thirteen years old now, May, correct?" I didn't answer. He knew how old I was. "Where along the line do you think you picked up such a blatant disrespect for authority?"

This was the eighth time this year that I'd been in Mr. Pringle's office. The last time was because I was involved in a food fight in the cafeteria. It hadn't been a big one—just a few Tater Tots hurled across the room at Jeremy Finkster, who'd thrown one at me first. Maybe a chocolate pudding, too. But Mr. Pringle had gone off on the whole disrespect for authority spiel during that visit too. It was his army thing. His "Give me five minutes, and I'll crush you like a bug" routine. I stared at the blue swirl pattern in the rug and jiggled my leg up and down.

"Do you have any idea where this attitude of yours is going to take you?" Mr. Pringle decided to try a different tactic. "Any idea at all? I'll tell you. Nowhere, young lady. Actually, I stand corrected. It *is* going to take you somewhere. It's going to take you to one big dead end. Period."

The swirls in the rug were actually a whole bunch of large and small paisley shapes, all crammed together. If I turned my head just a little to the right, they almost looked like they were moving. A great big sea of blue paisleys. Kind of cool.

Mr. Pringle pulled the cuff of his right shirt sleeve down over his wrist, and then the other. He picked a piece of lint off the front of his creased pants and tossed it in the trash can next to him. "Listen, I know you've had a tough year, Maeve. With everything that happened to your—"

"It's *May*!" It came out louder than I expected, more to drown out the rest of Mr. Pringle's sentence than to correct my name. Something tightened in the back of my throat, a pinpoint of pain, and I swallowed over it. "Could you pleaseplease*please* just call me May? Please. I hate the name Maeve."

Mr. Pringle rolled his bottom lip over his teeth. "Let's get to the real point of this meeting, shall we? I'm here to inform you that Miss Movado has agreed not to press charges."

"Wait, what?" My foot stopped jiggling. A flash of heat

spread out along my arms, all the way up to the back of my neck. "*Charges?* What kind of charges?"

"Defacing school property. Using foul and derogatory language in regard to a teacher."

"But I didn't *do* it!" I got up out of my chair, fists clenched at my side.

"You *did* do it." Mr. Pringle's voice was so sharp and so final that for a moment, I almost wavered. Almost. "*I* know you did it, and *you* know you did it. And we are not going to waste any more time going back and forth about it. You have two options. You can either be expelled—"

"Expelled?" I repeated. "I thought you just said Miss Movado wasn't going to press charges."

"She's isn't," Mr. Pringle answered coolly. "But I still can."

I sat back down again.

Mr. Pringle nodded. "I'm assuming you don't want to go that route."

I stared stoically at the rug. Shook my head the merest bit.

"All right then. These are your options: You can agree to expulsion from this school, *or* you can retake eighth-grade English with Miss Movado in summer school."

"Retake *English*?" I gripped the sides of the chair. "But I don't need to retake English! I didn't fail it!"

"That's not what Miss Movado seems to think."

Mr. Pringle turned slightly to the right, pressed a button on his phone, and then spoke into it. "All right, Lucille. Send Miss Movado in, please."

I swiveled around in my chair as the door opened. With her tiny head, wide hips, and stubby legs, it was not hard to imagine where the nickname Movado the Avocado had come from. It didn't help that her favorite color was green, either. The shirt she had on now was the same shade as celery, and her pants—a polyester blend that made a swiffing sound when she walked—were the color of limes. But Miss Movado's sad appearance belied her personality. She was the most feared—and hated—teacher in the whole school. She came down on students with a hurricane force. In her classroom, Movado the Avocado made Mr. Pringle look like Bo Peep. I couldn't imagine having to spend another *period* with her—let alone an entire summer. It would be the equivalent of torture.

Miss Movado gave Mr. Pringle a curt nod and sat down in the chair next to me.

"You failed me?" I stared at Movado the Avocado. "That is not fair! Is this like some kind of revenge?"

Movado the Avocado did not answer me. She stared straight ahead at the wall and blinked once.

"What would she need to get revenge for?" Mr. Pringle asked carefully.

"For . . ." I stumbled, trying to get my thoughts in order. "For not liking English or something, I guess!" Even I knew it sounded stupid, but it was all I could think of.

"This has nothing to do with not liking English." Movado the Avocado was still staring at the wall. "My job is not to get you to *like* English." Her voice was tight, but strangely soft. I leaned back in my chair a little. It was the first time I'd heard her talk in a normal tone of voice. Usually she was pacing around the classroom, roaring and yelling like some kind of deranged dinosaur.

"Then what'd you fail me for?"

Movado the Avocado turned her head so that she was looking directly at me. Her wide face was damp with perspiration. Small black hairs quivered along her upper lip, and a single curl clung like seaweed against her forehead. "To try again," she said. "The right way."

"To try *what* again?" I asked.

"All of it," Movado the Avocado said. "Technically, you did pass my class, May. By one point. The effort you put into the work I gave you all year was minimal at best, nonexistent at worst. I want you to do it again—with effort this time—the way you should have done it in the first place." Her voice was unnervingly quiet. It creeped me out.

"You can't *force* people to do things, you know." I sat

back and crossed my arms. "This is America. Land of the free, in case you haven't noticed."

"Oh, I've noticed," Movado the Avocado answered. "And you're perfectly free to choose whatever option Mr. Pringle just presented to you. Me or expulsion." She shrugged. "You'll just have to find another school to go to next year."

I glared at her. Narrowed my eyes at Mr. Pringle.

But no matter how hard I looked at both of them, the only thing I could see was the wide white sail of my eighth-grade summer slipping away.

Do you love the color pink?
All things sparkly? Mani/pedis?

These books are for you!

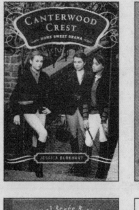

From Aladdin
Published by Simon & Schuster

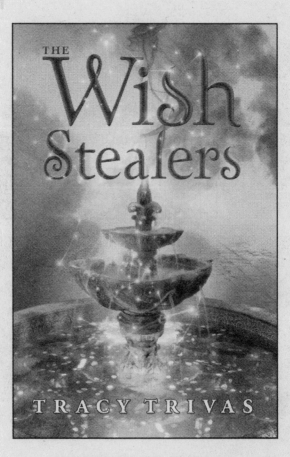

Enjoy this sweet treat from Aladdin!

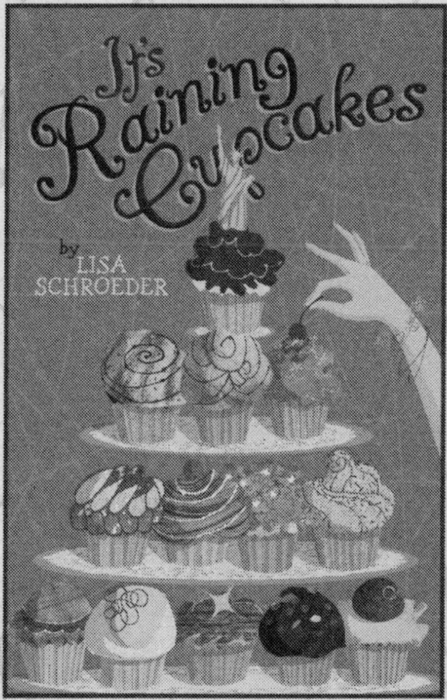

FROM ALADDIN

PUBLISHED BY SIMON & SCHUSTER